PRAISE FOR
LAST WORDS

"I didn't realize how much I missed seedy gritty corrupt crime-ridden New York City of the 1970s till I read Zahradnik's debut thriller. *Last Words* captures the palms-out politicians, the bully cops, the not-so-hapless homeless, the back-stabbing reporters of a city on the brink. The pace speeds up; the whispers and clues and leads all come together for a big empty-the-revolver and fling-the-vodka bottle finale. Well worth the trip back in time."
—Richard Zacks, author of *Island of Vice* and *Pirate Hunter*

"*Last Words* sizzles like the fuse on a powder keg. Hero reporter Coleridge Taylor is gritty and unstoppable as he plumbs the mean streets of New York City during its darkest days."
—Paul D'Ambrosio, author of *Easy* Selden Ring investigation prize ar medal finalist

"Rich Zahradnik is a superb craftsman. ᴸᶦᵏᵉ ᵃ adds layers of detail to a canvas he loves until he has created a picture that enthralls. Last Words has both beguiling landscape and revealing portraits and is a picture worth all its thousands of words: Rich in intrigue."
—Jeff Clark-Meads, author of *The Plowman* and *Tungol*

"In 1975, as New York City collapses into a financial and violent sinkhole, journalist Coleridge Taylor dodges bullets and bounds from borough to borough to find the killer of a seemingly homeless boy, a crime that the NYPD can't or won't solve. *The Bronx is Burning* meets *The Poet* in Rich Zahradnik's *Last Words*, a taut debut novel that keeps you guessing until the very end."
—Vito J. Racanelli, author and journalist

"Like any great crime thriller, *Last Words* keeps the pace frenetic, dangerous, and surprising at every turn. Zahradnik delivers an intelligent, flawed hero in Coleridge Taylor while showcasing the darkness of New York in the '70s that devoured the weak and unsuspecting. A visual, visceral debut from both the author and his lead crime reporter. I'm looking forward to more pulpy chapters."
—Diane Becker, Producer, FishBowl Films

"*Last Words* is as hard to put down as a grisly tabloid murder story. And indeed that's what the story is about. Despite his literary name, Coleridge Taylor is the 'Columbo' of beat reporters, suffering no fools and pursuing the facts at all costs. Set in 1975, the discovery of a deceased kid, presumed homeless, sets in motion Taylor's chilling odyssey."
—Claire Atkinson, senior media reporter, the *New York Post*

Last Words

Last Words

A Coleridge Taylor Mystery

RICH ZAHRADNIK

Seattle, WA

CAMEL PRESS

Camel Press
PO Box 70515
Seattle, WA 98127

For more information go to: www.Camelpress.com
www.richzahradnik.com

This is a work of fiction. Names, characters, places, brands,
media, and incidents are either the product of the author's
imagination or are used fictitiously.

Cover design by Sabrina Sun

Last Words
Copyright © 2014 by Rich Zahradnik

ISBN: 978-1-60381-207-8 (Trade Paper)
ISBN: 978-1-60381-208-5 (eBook)

Library of Congress Control Number: 2014942600

Printed in the United States of America

With love to my wife Sheri, who's
patiently waited the longest for this, and
my son Patrick, who's waited "forever."

———— ◆ ————

ACKNOWLEDGMENTS

———— ♦ ————

M Y SECOND NEWSPAPER job was as a freelancer for a newspaper in Westchester County, where I got paid to take obituaries over the phone for $10 a pop. I had a pretty low opinion of the work. That was until Meredith Halpern, a friend and colleague when I worked at CNN, pointed out the real craft of obits when written by the *New York Times*. Meredith's interest in obituaries started me musing on a writer's "what if": what if a top reporter were demoted to the kind of obituary grind I remembered from the early days of my career? Those were the first thoughts that led to *Last Words*.

Thanks also go to my agent, Dawn Dowdle of Blue Ridge Literary Agency, who believed in the manuscript and helped me make it better. Catherine Treadgold and Jennifer McCord, my editors at Camel Press, have been wonderful to work with and very understanding of a newbie to the book publishing process (which is nothing like publishing newspapers or magazines). Several people read *Last Words* in various stages, providing encouragement and helpful comments. Thank you to siblings Bob Zahradnik and Julie Zahradnik, sister-in-law Cathleen Zahradnik, and cousins John Murphy, Kevin

Murphy, and Rebecca Schmitz. Friends and fellow writers Nicole Valentine and Jim Banister were also good enough to give it a read, as was local fan Marianne Gilland.

Andrée Lockwood worked on an invaluable line-by-line edit of the manuscript before I went looking for an agent. My appreciation also goes to Jonathan Santlofer, director of The Center for Fiction's Crime Fiction Academy and bestselling mystery writer, for admitting me to the first class of the academy. It was the perfect moment to workshop the manuscript, and the edits he and my fellow students provided made the story better.

Finally, big thanks go to the reporters and editors of the *Colonial Times*, the student newspaper of Colonial Elementary School. I've been their advisor for the past four years. There are a lot of days when writing a novel doesn't go very well at all. The energy of those students made a bad writing day go away and gave me the energy to write again the next morning. This book isn't for kids, but those kids helped make it happen with their own enthusiasm for making a newspaper.

PART I:

Tuesday, March 11, 1975

1

———◆———

THE DEAD SITTING on his desk could wait.

Instead of going back to the office, Coleridge Taylor stopped at the newsstand on 23rd Street and looked at the front page of the *Daily News*. MAYHEM IN QUEENS spelled out in two-inch type. Another story that should have been his. The *Times* led with a dull speech by President Ford. It made him miss Nixon. Nothing like a crook in the White House to sell papers. He spent a nickel on a pack of Teaberry gum, folded a stick into his mouth, pulled his field jacket tight against the wind, and turned east toward Bellevue.

Taylor spent his long lunches making the rounds—precincts, ERs, firehouses—the same rounds he'd done when he was the paper's top police reporter, before they'd banished him to obits. Unless he caught a break soon, his career would be over. He'd be a has-been at thirty-four. As he walked, Taylor rapped his pen on his notebook, a nervous habit that kicked in when he was looking for a story, and now he was running out of time. In a week, Worth and Marmelli were going to review the work he'd done since his demotion and decide. A permanent job writing obituaries or back out on the street. He didn't know which was worse, but if he kept dodging obit duty, that meeting wasn't going to go so well.

Gusts off the East River buffeted him as his long strides carried him up First Avenue. His arms were long, too, while his high cheekbones and strong jawline added to the impression that Taylor was all angles. He slipped the notebook and pen into his coat and stuffed his big hands into his pockets. Bellevue towered over FDR Drive and the muck-brown East River. He went up the driveway to the ER entrance.

The waiting room was empty. Unusual for New York's medical center of last resort. The nurse behind the reception desk, Barbara Cortez, was a bit on the chubby side and smiled no matter what she had to deal with.

"Anything good?" He leaned in.

Cortez was one of those women who looked better the closer you got because of her kind dark eyes and smooth olive skin. "We're going to be busy in about ten minutes. Three kids up in Harlem. All gun-shot."

"What happened?"

"A detective sees a kid pull a knife at 131st and Lenox. He shoots. More shots. We've got another race riot."

This sent a jolt through Taylor's gut. "They're driving them all the way downtown? What's wrong with Harlem Hospital?"

"The cops ordered it. They didn't want protestors going over there and making things worse."

"Ten blocks versus more than a hundred? Those kids could die." Taylor took out his notebook and wrote down the intersection and what Cortez had said about the order to bring the boys downtown. He circled this last fact. If something stuck out, he noted it.

"I just treat whoever gets here alive." Cortez shrugged. "I thought you were doing death notices."

"Obits."

"Aren't they the same?"

"One you pay for. One you don't."

Taylor headed down the corridor, away from the ER. Few things bothered him more than walking away from a big story. Cops shooting black kids was a very big story, and every police reporter in town would soon descend on the ER. He couldn't be there when they did.

The gray hospital walls matched his mood as he wound an aimless route around the hallways and ended up in a back corridor. A black orderly, tall with graying hair, pushed a gurney with a body under a sheet in the other direction.

"That one of the boys from Harlem?"

"No. This one's white and no cop shot him. Young. Homeless. Found dead on the street."

"How'd he die?"

"Like I said, homeless." The orderly stopped pushing.

"That's not a cause of death."

"What it's been for five others in the past two weeks. This wicked March freeze is catching them all off guard."

"*Five*? Dead from exposure?"

"That's right. I've got to get this one into the cutting room." The orderly pushed past, and Taylor followed him into the autopsy room.

"Where do you think you're going?"

"I'm going to write about this kid."

"The homeless don't get stories in the paper."

"First time for everything."

The orderly rolled the gurney onto an elevator. Taylor stepped on, too. The orderly read his press pass. It expired in three months, and if Taylor couldn't get back on the police beat by then, he'd lose it and all the access it gave him. Doors all over the city would slam shut. The thought chilled him.

"Coleridge Samuel Taylor."

"Just Taylor." He hated the literary ornamentation of his name.

"Name's Jackson."

The autopsy room looked like any operating theater with its

silver-domed lights, trolleys of medical instruments and glass-fronted metal cabinets. The acrid smell of disinfectant was even stronger here.

A second orderly came in and helped Jackson shift the wrapped body onto a table, both of them grunting.

"Jesus, this body is frozen stiff," Jackson said.

The second orderly shrugged and left, as if moving bodies was his only job.

"You said he died of exposure, right?" Taylor leaned in.

"Yeah, but he feels like …." The orderly frowned. "The last time a body came in frozen solid like this was when a jumper went into the Hudson back in January." He pulled the sheets open near the neck. The corpse was still dressed and the orderly fingered the material of the outer clothing. "The coat and sweater are cold but *not* frozen." He slid his hand inside the sweater. "The undershirt feels like it's iced right to him. The skin *is* frozen."

"That doesn't make sense." Taylor looked from the orderly to the body on the slab. "It's like he froze from the inside out. Or his outer clothes were put on *after* he froze." He made a note of this. "Be interesting to hear what the pathologist makes of it."

"Not much if he thinks he's cutting a homeless boy. How are you going to do a story on a dead nobody?" The orderly sighed and turned away.

I'll find out what makes him a somebody. Getting frozen in your underwear and dressed by another person might do the trick.

"You gotta be a big somebody to get your death notice in the papers here."

This victim's story already bothered him. The boy was going to disappear. Taylor was watching it happen. No last words for the family. No notice taken anywhere by anyone. It had happened before, with Billy. This was going on now in Taylor's city. There was no excuse for it.

"When did the body come in?"

"Night watch. Three, four in the morning."

"You're just now rolling him in?"

"No room at the inn. Kept the body outside in the ambulance."

"What if they got another call?"

"Couldn't. No one to replace the driver going off shift. Poor bastards had to take a cab back to their house. These budget cuts are just crazy. So we kept him cold out there. The guys just came back to get their wagon."

"Where'd they pick him up?"

"The Meatpacking District." Jackson looked at the body again. "I'll tell you one thing. I doubt they'll be cutting today. It's going to take a whole shift to defrost him. Very strange. Or plain bad luck."

Only the facts interested Taylor. They'd explain how this boy froze from the inside out, the cause and effect. Nothing unlucky. Nothing strange.

Jackson pulled off the sheet. The dead boy wore an army field jacket similar to Taylor's. Threads hung at the edges of the rectangle above the left breast pocket where a name patch should have been.

"Whatever the name tag said, it wasn't this kid's," Taylor said. "He's too young for the military." *Could be the father's*, Taylor thought. *Or maybe the boy bought it at the Army & Navy.* Taylor would check all that out. The jacket had seen a lot of wear and tear. Some of that might be from life on the street.

"Now that I think of it," Jackson said, "it looks like the one I got when I fought in Europe. You don't see these as much. Thing never was warm enough."

Jackson was right. The boy's jacket featured lapels instead of a circular collar and the fabric looked thinner. The kid wore dungarees, patched the length of both legs, more patches than jean material really. The "V" of a blue sweater, probably wool, showed under the jacket.

Jackson nodded at Taylor's jacket. "You a vet?"

"No."

"Just like the look?"

"No." The implication stung, as if his was a fashion statement. His brother, trained to fight somewhere cold in Europe, was ordered to Vietnam. Billy didn't need the heavy jacket, or didn't want to pack it, or had wanted to leave something behind with his older brother. Taylor wasn't sure which. He gave it to Taylor and never came back. Maybe because of the question, the teenager became his brother Billy for a moment. Another kid forever lost to his family. The boy was the same height, though slighter and younger. What was younger when you were dead?

The orderly was saying something, forcing Billy's face to fade, replaced by that of the dead boy. This face was smooth, without lines, and the nose straight. His lips were full, almost pouting, and his gray eyes looked directly into the bright overhead lights, unblinded and blind. His hair was thick, long and clean, which was odd. If this kid was homeless, it should have been matted and dirty.

"Look at this." Jackson pointed to the jacket's right sleeve.

More than twenty national flags were sewn down the outside of the right arm of the field jacket, from the shoulder to the cuff. France, Italy, USA, East Germany, Canada, the USSR, West Germany, Red China, and some countries Taylor couldn't identify.

Taylor walked around the table. "Same on this side. No unit or rank. Those were cut away a long time ago. Just more flags. It's like the UN."

Thousands of army field jackets hung in the closets of New York vets, the families of the dead and even ex-hippies, but none would look like this one. Taylor knew people would remember it. This was starting to look like a story he could follow.

Jackson left the room. Taylor checked the boy's left hand, leaned in to get closer and used his Bic pen to lift the fingers. They were smooth, almost feminine, with telltale signs of civilized living—clean, well-trimmed fingernails. Not a speck of dirt under any of them. The fingers on the right hand were the same. This kid wasn't homeless, or hadn't been for long. The field jacket would lead to someone who knew him, who could tell his story. He listed the countries of the flags he could ID and descriptions of those he couldn't.

"I thought we were rid of you, Taylor." Dr. R. Martin Quirk, the assistant coroner, stood inside the door. Taylor looked from Quirk's long face to the stubby fingers that seemed imperfect instruments for prodding inside bodies, even dead ones.

"This kid wasn't homeless," Taylor said.

"What do you know? Don't turn this John Doe into another of your page one specials. I've got six homicides in the cooler, bodies piling up in the emergency room—high priority, cops shooting civilians—and five accidentals, old people who froze to death in their apartments. I've got to cut them all anyway. They won't let me put 'unpaid Con Ed bill' as cause on the death certificate."

"Will you at least check the 'missing' list?"

Quirk always claimed to be overworked, but he was just plain lazy.

"That's a cop's job."

"They won't."

"I'm not their master, thank Christ. Why don't *you* do it? You're the reporter."

Taylor decided not to disabuse him of that notion. From his jacket's right pocket, he pulled out and opened the collapsible Polaroid he carried for capturing a scene when a click was faster than taking notes. A snap-flash and Taylor held the instant photo, a black square until it developed. In two minutes, chemicals and metals would resolve into a color picture of the dead boy's face. He needed it to track down who the kid was.

"I'll call you to get cause of death." He put the developing picture in his coat pocket next to his wallet and went straight through the double doors without glancing back.

Why didn't the boy show the wear and tear of rough living? He might have been a recent arrival on the street, a runaway who didn't bargain on the freezing weather and died almost as soon as he ran. A sad story. Newspaper readers loved sad stories, even if they said they didn't.

He decided to go to Bellevue's main entrance to avoid the chaos of the ER and the reporters who must be there by now. Jack Fahey, his replacement, would rat him out to the editors at the *Messenger-Telegram*. Fahey had gotten where he was now by being Worth's newsroom stooge.

The hallway's fluorescent lights hummed and flickered on, off, on, off. Pine Sol, piss, and hospital food filled the air. Two patients appeared to be sleeping on gurneys in the hall. At least he hoped they were sleeping. Not a nurse or doctor in sight. They were all in the ER now, no doubt. It was Taylor's great hope, should bad luck or mischief befall him, that he remain conscious long enough to whisper to the ambulance driver, "Anywhere but Bellevue."

To clear his head of the smells, he put a fresh piece of Teaberry gum in his mouth. The minty-licorice flavor helped some as he came out onto the street. The wind had died down. He took out the Polaroid snapshot, shook it a couple of times, and examined the kid's face.

No, the boy didn't look a thing like his brother. Why did this surprise him? Probably because Billy remained a teenager in Taylor's memory, rather than the tall muscular soldier who left for Nam in '73 at the age of twenty-two. Enlisting as a grunt had been the perfect rebellion against their father, who was the intellectual, the screamer of Coleridge's poetry. Taylor had never known how to express the pain of Billy's loss. It was a black, hard lump deep inside him. He was afraid of what would happen if he did anything but just let it sit there. So, he never tried. He slipped the picture back in his pocket.

Taylor brushed his hand through his short brown hair to put it back into a rough part. He'd tried growing it long to match the current trend, but felt it looked like a dirty mop as soon as the hair got past his ears. So it was cut to the same length he'd worn it at ever since outgrowing a boyhood crew cut.

His stomach made a grumbling noise, a complaint Taylor ignored. His body might think he needed to eat, but he had no interest. He'd lost interest in food after he'd written the story that got him demoted two months ago. Tonight he had work to do on his own time, and he needed to get his damn obits done first. Coffee would go down nice; he'd grab that on the way up to the paper.

Five-foot piles of rock-hard grimy snow walled the sidewalk from the street. The *Messenger-Telegram's* offices were four broad avenues away, between Park and Lex, a pleasant walk across 28th Street if New York weren't in the grip of the freeze. Taylor hiked his collar up. The other pedestrians were muffled in heavy overcoats and parkas, scarves and hats. He should have put on something like that, instead of Billy's jacket. This morning he'd considered longjohns but couldn't find any in the disarray of the Airstream trailer. He woke later than his usual late and rushed to get dressed, once he realized—with a loud curse—that the hot water heater was on the fritz. Should he get the water heater fixed? That might delay repair work on his house, and he was spending everything he could on that.

Six months ago, he'd broken the story on a ring of corrupt detectives on the Harlem vice squad and received a Molotov cocktail through the window as thanks. He needed to get out of the damn trailer in his driveway. His neighbors were running out of patience.

2

———◆———

THE *MESSENGER-TELEGRAM* WAS the Frankenstein's monster of New York newspapers. Part *Daily Telegram*, part *New York Messenger* and part *Morning Star*, all grafted together in a bid to survive declining readership, white flight to the suburbs and the greatest newspaper killer of them all, TV news. The *New York Journal-American*, the *New York Herald Tribune* and eight other papers had died by '67. Of course, everyone knew the *Times* would go on forever, and the *Daily News* would go on as long as there was a borough of Queens. But the *MT*—spelled *Empty* by the wise guys at the *Village Voice*—owed its financial survival to the Garfield family and the New Haven Life Insurance Company.

In the lobby of the New Haven Life Building, Taylor stopped in Frieda's, ordered coffee—two creams, two sugars—and took a long sip. The warm creamy drink fooled his stomach and stopped the growling.

Next stop, Cranston's, a newsstand that had papers from all over the country in neat stacks, pile after pile. Taylor reviewed them. Nameplates, headlines, pictures, stories. Studying the way various papers played a crime, who was claiming a scoop, what held the fascination of people in other cities. He picked up the *Des Moines Register* and checked out a triple homicide. Violent death in the Midwest seemed out of place to him.

He took the elevator up and it opened on the huge newsroom occupying the entire tenth floor. The perfect space to house a couple hundred insurance salesman, or in this case, journalists. He made his way through a bewildering maze of desks, partitions, bookcases, support pillars, file cabinets, wood and glass offices built in seemingly random locations, typewriter tables and chairs owned by no specific desk. The staff of the paper moved in two years ago after a desperate merger. A tremendous amount of crap had filled the space, like the way a coral reef sprung up without any plan. The clutter made the room seem even larger than it was because you couldn't see the outer walls. Most visitors got lost after they turned a couple of corners.

Taylor could walk the newsroom blind, knew it as a map of territories and influence. Actual offices meant position. Their proximity to Editor-in-Chief Oscar Garfield equaled real power. He wound his way to the City Desk outside Garfield's glass office amid the clattering of typewriters, the keys struck at different speeds and in different rhythms—an uneven rolling noise, a kind of newsroom surf that energized him every time he heard it.

City Editor Bradford J. Worth Jr., one of five men sitting inside a horseshoe of pushed-together desks, marked copy with a pencil, skimming over lines, correcting, cutting words, adding his own, slashing paragraphs. He moved on to the next page, ignoring the shadow Taylor cast across his desk. Taylor wasn't surprised. Everyone under the city editor lived by the man's schedule and whims. Taylor knew how to wait. Every story, in the end, was about waiting. Finally, the pencil halted and the city editor looked up. "What?" Which meant, *Go away*.

Worth's features were fine and precise, as if their owner had edited them himself. He was younger than he looked or acted.

Three years younger than Taylor, in fact, and ambitious in a predatory way. He had risen rapidly through the newsroom without ever going out on the street to report a story.

"Got a story idea for you, Chief."

"I'm not your goddamned chief. Marmelli's your boss now. There are no ideas in obituaries. Only the dead."

Worth tapped the eraser rapidly on the paper. Taylor leaned on the corner of the desk. Worth hated people touching any part of the pristine maple surface. His inbox was filled with an evenly stacked pile. The out box was empty. That was it, except for the copy Worth was editing, and as Taylor slid a bit farther, a chunk of ass.

Having a lead made Taylor reckless, as if he'd already won his job back. "Don't want to write it, just see that it gets covered. I heard something about a police shooting in Harlem."

Worth fixed light blue eyes on Taylor, a pucker of skin above his nose the beginning of a frown. "Fahey's on it. I don't have time for this. Or you."

"The cops ordered all the kids taken to Bellevue to avoid a demonstration at Harlem Hospital. Some kids probably died because of that decision."

"Fahey knows what the hell he's doing. Five kids shot. One dead so far. A cop stabbed. A riot still ongoing. That's more than enough story for him to worry about. If I find out you're doing anything but obits, you'll be out *before* next Monday."

Taylor slid off the desk and shook his head. "A man in a newsroom who doesn't want to hear about news."

"I warned you." Worth spoke with cool pleasure.

Taylor wound his way to Obituaries, a distant principality in the windowless southeast corner of the newsroom, as far from the center of power as it was possible to get. The other desk was unoccupied. Lou Marmelli, like the undertakers he dealt with, kept civil, bankers' hours, while Taylor refused to change from the schedule of a police reporter, showing up late in the morning and not leaving until the bulldog edition came off the presses. That was one of the many reasons Marmelli disliked him.

Two pink "While You Were Out" slips were taped to his phone. After he was taken off the police beat, his message count had plummeted from a pad a day to this. One was from his carpenter, Mahoney, who either wanted a payment or had found another problem. Calls from Mahoney were never good news. The other was from Laura Wheeler, the second of the day. "Stop dodging me. You owe me a lunch." Laura worked the police beat, and was in fact the first woman assigned to cops since World War II.

The neat script on the message slip made him think of Laura and her warm brown eyes. Intelligence. Concern. Laughter. Those eyes had knocked the chip off. He'd dropped his prejudice against her Columbia degree and Upper Eastside connections and asked her to lunch the day he finished the front-page story on a nine-year-old heroin addict. It was supposed to be a celebration, but the next day the little girl disappeared, along with the cop who arranged the interview. Taylor had been set up. Newsroom scandal, the paper's retraction, and his demotion followed.

He wasn't going to sit with her now, the big failure banished to Obituaries. It was a large newsroom, maybe not large enough to avoid her forever, but he was giving it a try. He snapped the message slip once with his finger and tossed it.

Marmelli left three late deaths for him to deal with—Park Avenue proctologist, city councilman who served in the '50s, and society matron. He wrote those in an hour, running on autopilot.

After that, he pulled out his notebook and reviewed the national flags sewn onto the field jacket the dead boy wore. There was no pattern in the arrangement of the flags that he could see. This was an odd death. The John Doe might have died the quiet dream of hypothermia, if you ignored the fact his clothes appeared to have been soaked in water and frozen to him. Had that happened before or after he died? How? What was the kid doing in the Meatpacking District? There were no shelters down there. He considered the clean fingernails and the five other homeless people killed on the street by the bitter cold. Billy's memory kept intruding, that hard black thing deep down inside. He snapped the notebook shut. The only dead kid he could do anything about was the teenager in the morgue—the one who interested nobody as either a police case or a news story. What he didn't know was how to get it in the paper. Still, he had to *get it* first. The teen might have been involved in drugs or prostitution. He'd talk to a guy he knew who worked Eighth Avenue. This was the hard slog of reporting, but oh how he loved it. He was on to something that could become a story.

He made a few calls to old sources and learned only that no one wanted to talk to the ex-top police reporter. He checked the wire printers on the way out.

SAIGON, March 10, 1975 (UPI)—The city of Ban Me Thout fell today to the army of North Vietnam in what appears to be a full-scale invasion of South Vietnam.

The foreign desk had done little with the story since the North came over the border. Tomorrow he planned to talk to Roger Novak, the foreign editor. He wanted the story to get the play his brother's sacrifice deserved. That was concrete; getting something in the paper was something he knew how to do.

He left the paper at seven-thirty. Tonight, for starters, he needed to see a homeless man named Harry Jansen.

3

———◆———

TAYLOR TOOK THE No. 6 train to Grand Central, changed to the No. 7 to get to Port Authority and walked the rest of the way into Hell's Kitchen. Snow fell heavy and fast, covering the sidewalk and reducing visibility to less than a block. The pedestrian traffic thinned to nothing and the cars dwindled as he walked west on 47th, crossing 11th Avenue. A massive hulk resolved into the half-completed West Side Freight Terminal, a Mayor Lindsay project that was conceived to bring blue-collar jobs back to the neighborhood. It was abandoned early in the city's fiscal crisis. Instead of jobs, it now offered shelter to those who had none.

Taylor stopped at a heavy plastic sheet that served as a door, pushed it aside, entered and tucked the plastic back into place under a cinderblock. Bed sheets, canvas, plywood, plastic—any kind of material that could be scrounged—had been draped over the lower skeleton of the unfinished building. The wind banged the plastic sheets, making a cracking, snapping sound.

The passage opened into a bigger space. People breathed and shifted against one another. A large ring of cinderblocks stacked two and three high circled a bonfire fed on pieces of lumber.

A four-by-four tumbled from the top of the fire, exploding into hot coals and embers. Sparks formed a constellation, rose and winked out before they reached the darkness above. Sitting figures crowded three deep around the flames, sharing the warmth of bodies and the fire. Wood smoke mixed with human musk. Showers were something else this makeshift homeless shelter didn't offer.

The plastic at the back wall banged some more, a sail hit by a gust. The draft blew the smoke at Taylor. The odor of tar and burning plastic caught at the back of his throat. He blinked his eyes and stepped to the left.

"Taylor of the *New York Messenger-Telegram*. It has been some time." The deep voice came from the other side of the fire circle. "We were ... I don't know how to put it. *Amazed* is wrong, since Sammy *was* beaten to death. Impressed? Shocked? You wrote about his murder in your paper. Forced the police to investigate. They even arrested the guy. We die all the time. No one takes notice."

"Murders should always be investigated."

"Controversial view in the city of New York." Taylor caught Harry Jansen's hint of a smile through the shimmering hot air above the fire. Jansen was dressed as Taylor had last seen him. Dark blue overcoat, gray morning coat and charcoal slacks— the suit you rented for a wedding. Taylor moved around the ring of blocks toward Jansen. The fire appeared in miniature in Jansen's large green eyes. "We *bought* copies. To keep in his memory. What was the point of putting those stories in your newspaper?"

"It's not *my* paper. Like I said when I first visited—"

"I read the paper every day. I don't see your byline anymore."

"I was reassigned. No bylines for obits." It embarrassed Taylor to say it out loud, even here. That just brought on guilt. These people had bigger problems than he'd ever known.

"None of us died today," said Jansen.

"There's a dead boy at Bellevue. Looks homeless. Looks like he froze to death."

"What do you mean 'looks'?"

"No ID. No autopsy yet."

"Right now, freezing to death is easier than going for a walk."

"Six, counting this kid."

"Six? Six. It's that bad."

Taylor reached inside his jacket and pulled out the Polaroid headshot.

"Does he look familiar?" Taylor offered the photo. "He was found in the Meatpacking District."

"He's not homeless."

The response came too quick. He needed Jansen to be sure. "Look at it. I have to know."

Jansen held up the picture. "Don't know him. If he was in the Gansevoort Market, no way he's homeless. No shelters. No overpasses. It's a bad neighborhood at night. Worse in the day, if that's possible."

"Doesn't mean he couldn't have ended up there."

"The neighborhood's Mafia controlled. We negatively impact upon their quality of life. We're not even allowed to walk through. They don't move you along with a little prod like Officer O'Billyclub. They beat on you hard."

"Maybe this kid," Taylor pointed to the picture, "didn't know any better and ended up down there."

"All the people on the street know better. He wasn't homeless if he was found there."

"Everyone else look, please." Taylor handed it to the person nearest in the circle and the picture started its way around the fire.

"No."

"Nope."

"Man, so young. Don't know him."

All nos. Taylor took the shot when it came back.

"How did he die?" Jansen asked.

"Oddly. It looks like he was soaked in water, maybe before he died. His underclothes were frozen to him. He wore an army field jacket. I'm sure it's the key to his identity. The arms are covered in flags up and down both sleeves."

"Voichek?" Fear entered Jansen's eyes. "Let me see that picture." He looked at it again. "I don't know this boy. Why would he have on Voichek's jacket?"

"You're sure it's Voichek's?"

"Without seeing it, pretty sure. Mark Voichek's been wearing one with all these flags on the sleeves since World War II. It doesn't make any sense. He'd never give it away."

"Spell the last name." Jansen did and Taylor wrote it in his notebook. "Did he own heavily patched jeans and a blue V-neck sweater?"

"Don't know about the sweater, but he had jeans like that. A lot of people on the street do."

Here was the real beginning. A scoop started with a lead. That little item, scrap of evidence, bit of hearsay that set him on the chase. That was why he loved this job. The thrill when a hunch proved true and every question took him closer to breaking the story.

"Why all the flags?"

"Voichek said this to me once, and only once, 'I fought the war that won the peace and created the great United Nations. I had a hand in that.' Sounds goofy these days, but he was serious. Said it was the most important thing he'd done in his life. So he put all those flags on his sleeves. He won two Purple Hearts and a Bronze Star fighting in Africa and Italy. Never wore those. Never talked about it again. A real-live hero hiding with the rest of us on the street."

"Where's he now?"

"I don't know."

Taylor looked up from the notebook.

"Means nothing." Jansen spoke with an edge, his usual confidence gone. "He doesn't always stay here. Except for five years in the army, he was an honest-to-God hobo—riding the rails during the Great Depression, through the fifties and sixties, right up until a few years ago. He finally stopped in New York because they padlocked the boxcars. There's no one better at surviving on the streets."

"I'd worry now. This dead boy showed up dressed in a jacket you say Voichek wouldn't part with. That's not a good sign. Either he was involved—"

"Never! Something twisted has happened. You said you're writing obituaries now. Why are you bothering with this?"

Taylor put his faith in the connections. The kid had on Voichek's clothing. The body was found in a neighborhood the homeless didn't dare enter. The kid and Voichek were connected somehow. The why of it all, that was for later. The who first. Who's the killer? Who's the kid? He needed to ID the victim before worrying about the motive.

"It's a story." *They can't ignore a good story, not even Worthless.* Whack, Whack, WHACK!

A loud racket from outside the shelter. The room went quiet. Whack, Whack, WHACK!

"It's the Street Sweepers." Jansen spoke with urgent authority. "We need to move. Let's go! Out the back way, everyone. Grab your things along the hall and follow your division leaders. They just want to scare us. Keep to the plan and no one will get hurt."

The bundles sitting around the fire rose and ghosted out of the room in drilled fashion. The banging got louder, lost all of its rhythm and became a crashing noise. The plastic on the 47th Street side of the uncompleted freight terminal took two heavy blows and fell to the ground.

Taylor spoke to Jansen as he passed. "Who are the Street Sweepers?"

"A gang. They don't like homeless people. They've chased us away before. Come with us."

"I'll stay. Sounds like another good story to me."

"We'll be on the pier with all the old railroad ties. Find me when they're done here, if you're not done in first."

Jansen was gone.

Three men wearing motorcycle pants and jackets, leather shining in the firelight, stepped over the fallen plastic into the main room of the shelter. Each held a trash can lid and a different weapon—a baseball bat, an ax, and a sledgehammer. Red bandannas covered their faces. They kept up the racket on the lids with their weapons, as if trying to scare away animals in the forest.

Taylor's stomach tightened into a small, hard knot. He'd nailed some of his best stories scared out of his wits. This was at least a good story. Masked men chasing the homeless into the arctic night. Okay, a great story. But was having no plan at all really the best plan?

The man with the bat held it straight up in the air, and the noise stopped. "John Henry, check down that hallway. See if any of them stayed behind." Lowering the bat, he stepped around the fire and over to Taylor. "Lookie here, Mr. Bunyan."

"What's that, Mr. Ruth?" asked the one with the ax.

"We've got a hero tonight. After we warned 'em never to come back."

"Do you mean the poor homeless folks you frightened into the night? Oh, they definitely split, and fast," said Taylor. "Scared shitless, I'd say. Why are you doing this to them?"

Mr. Bunyan started chopping the bonfire apart with his ax. The light in the big space dimmed as he did. Pieces of burning lumber tumbled onto left-behind blankets, starting small, smoky fires. Mr. Bunyan didn't seem to notice because he was so focused on destruction.

"Hey, man, we got one of them crazy vets." Mr. Ruth shouldered the bat. "Why do all you guys dress like you're still in the fucking jungle?"

"Not a veteran. Just a boring, old-fashioned newspaper reporter." Taylor flipped open his notebook. He loved the power of a little pad to silence all sorts of assholes. "So you guys are the Street Sweepers. Is that a gang name?"

Mr. Ruth smacked the bat into the palm of a leather glove. "What we're doing is none of your fucking business."

"Really? Big brave men like you beating up on the homeless. You must want publicity for that."

Mr. Ruth poked him hard in the chest with the bat, knocking him back a step. So much for the intimidating power of his notebook. "These scum are ruining our city. They need to get the hell out."

The end of the bat slammed into the crook of Taylor's shoulder. Pain shot down his arm. The guy was really starting to piss him off.

"Beating up reporters gets secret groups and their secret names in the newspapers. All the newspapers."

"Fuck you." Mr. Ruth wound up for a batter's swing at Taylor's head. He ducked under the wild arc. An opening. One, two to the groin. Mr. Ruth dropped the bat and bent to the ground, clutching his balls and groaning.

Mr. Bunyan quit chopping and advanced on Taylor. Retreat now looked like the best option. He picked up Mr. Ruth's bat and threw it spinning into the remains of the fire; sparks jumped as it landed. This froze his attacker for an instant, giving Taylor the seconds he sought to turn and bolt into the darkness behind, going for the back door Jansen and his people had used.

Paul Bunyan took up the challenge, yelling as he came.

Taylor made it five yards and caught his foot on something hard and heavy. He fell, scraping his knee badly on a cinderblock. Blood wet his torn wool pants.

Mr. Bunyan closed the distance.

Taylor rolled onto his back and fumbled for his brother's last gift—given on his final home leave after a couple of mobsters threatened Taylor over a story—the pistol he wore in a holster strapped at his left ankle.

He pulled at the gun but forgot to unhook the strap holding it in place. He yanked twice at the leather to release the catch. This was crazy. Why the hell did anyone use an ankle holster?

Mr. Bunyan raised the ax.

The strap came free and Taylor twisted the revolver, took a breath, pulled it straight out and rolled left as the blunt end of the ax head hit the concrete where he'd been. Sparks flew. The thing would have crushed his skull.

He pointed high over Mr. Bunyan's silhouette and fired. He'd never practiced with the thing, had absolutely no aim and was lucky he didn't kill the man he was trying to scare.

In the dim light of what was left of the fire, Mr. Bunyan froze, ax high. Mr. Ruth was still prone. A gun changed everything for these bullies.

"Enough of this." Taylor got to his feet and circled left so both men were a good ten feet from him.

"John Henry!" Silence. Mr. Ruth yelled the name again louder and the third man appeared.

"Now, boys, if you'll exit the way you came, this costume party is over."

The men left, walking backward, eyes on Taylor and the gun. Mr. Ruth, the last, gingerly stepped over the plastic, one hand still on his crotch. Taylor crept up to the gaping hole, gripping the pistol, his knuckles white. The men disappeared into the snowy blackness.

Taylor went to the pier to retrieve Jansen and his people.

"You surprise me again." Jansen stamped out the last burning blanket. "Do you deal death with one hand and write it with the other?"

"Hardly." He shifted his gaze to the people putting the tarps and plastic back up. He was embarrassed. He hated thrusting himself into the middle of the story. "They weren't interested in interviews. I didn't like the odds."

"I pray they don't return."

"Why are they harassing you?"

"It's a fucking ugly world."

"I was looking for a specific motive."

"I don't have it for you. We have few fans."

"Do you think the Street Sweepers are killers?"

"You mean the boy?"

"Yes. It could be murder. Maybe it was them?"

"They've threatened us and wrecked the shelter. I see them as bullies, and bullies are cowards."

"Cowards wouldn't mind odds of three against one. Particularly if one was a teenager. Anyone who attacks the homeless is a suspect in the kid's death."

"I told you he wasn't homeless."

"What if someone *thought* he was?"

Jansen might be willing to dismiss the idea. Taylor couldn't. That gang was dangerous. If the kid turned out to be a murder victim, he'd need to find out who the Street Sweepers really were. He took out his notebook and leafed through the pages. His pulse had slowed down to near normal, but the gun tugged at his left ankle like a warm iron weight. Time to get back on track. To *get* the story, not *be* the story. "How can I find Voichek?"

"I expected you'd ask. I'll offer you a deal of a sort. We have another missing person, and I'm worried about him. He's not someone who should be away this long. If you'll check your sources, we'll get Voichek in touch with you."

"Why the runaround? Just tell me where to find Voichek."

"I don't know where he is. He's out there somewhere. We'll see him or hear of him long before you can check all the places the homeless go. Joshua Harper, on the other hand, doesn't have Voichek's survival skills. He's been missing for four days. I'm worried about him. When you arrived tonight, I thought you'd come about him." Jansen made Taylor sound like the Angel of Death.

He didn't like it. "I still don't see—"

"What if Joshua's another victim? I'm talking about checking the police and hospitals. The morgue too. All those people you know. Joshua can't survive out there. You check your sources, and we'll find Voichek."

"Do you suspect a crime?" Taylor looked at Jansen.

The hobo chief slowly shook his head. "I don't know what to suspect."

"What can you tell me that'll help me track him down?"

"He had a wife named Marion and a son he wrote to, at least for a while. He mentioned he worked a job until two years ago."

"Where?"

"A place in the Bronx." Jansen reached into the pocket of his long coat, pulled out a book, and handed it to Taylor. "He did that."

The binding didn't have a title or publisher. The cover was stamped in gold embossed type: Graham Book Bindery, New York City, est. 1894. Inside, blank pages. The weight and quality of the paper stock varied throughout the book, heavy coated to tissue-thin. It must be some kind of sample. The cover leaf listed an address: 325 E. 139th St., The Bronx, N.Y. Joshua Harper's name was written on the inside cover, in a flowing cursive that was almost calligraphy.

Taylor noted down the company name and address and the wife's name and circled that twice. "What does he look like?"

"Five foot eleven, skinny, with curly black hair and blue eyes. He wears a black parka and brown work pants."

"That helps."

"So, we have an agreement? You'll find Joshua. We'll let you know when Voichek turns up."

"I'll be in touch. Call me if you hear anything—*anything*—about Voichek. Or if anyone else goes missing or is attacked."

Taylor walked toward the doorway to the outside. One of the homeless, a smaller bundle in the shadows, cried out, "Good night, John-boy!"

Taylor reached for the plastic tarp.

The same voice, almost a whisper, "Good night, John-boy."

The unfinished freight terminal fell back into the snowy darkness as he walked east on 48th at a little past eleven. The .32 was warm against his left ankle, and with its presence as a goad, he picked up the pace. After his fumbling encounter with the Street Sweepers, he was pretty sure he couldn't get the gun out fast enough if he were attacked in this neighborhood where muggings were the least of the crimes.

He tried a pay phone at Seventh Avenue, next to a combo peep show/porn shop. No dial tone. A barker in front of the show waved at him like he had a secret to share.

The flashing, dancing signs of Times Square were turned off because of the energy crisis, replaced by plain old billboards, and the light that remained at the Crossroads of the World was a kind of dusk-at-night. He took the stairs down to the R train. On the subway ride, he considered his deal with Jansen. He didn't mind the extra work. He traded information all the time. Jansen just might be right: his people would find Voichek faster out among the homeless. Besides, he had other work. Checking missing persons to try to ID the dead kid. That would now serve double duty since he could see if anything had been reported on Harper as well. Maybe there was a pattern with these homeless deaths? Real digging required there.

He rode the R to Queens, got off at the Forest Hills-71st Avenue stop and arrived at his house on Fleet Street just before midnight. The place looked little changed from the night of the fire six months earlier. Scorch marks gave all the windows angry black eyebrows. A third of the roof was gone, covered by a tarp. The wind drove against it, making the same cracking sound as at the homeless shelter. He'd spent fifteen hundred so far on Maloney and Maloney. They told him they were doing important structural work under the roof. Hearing that didn't cheer him up. It would go quicker if he could spend more. He couldn't.

Inside the 20-year-old Airstream in the driveway, he sat on the narrow bed that doubled as a seat in the kitchenette-cum-bedroom. He turned on the radio and opened the half-sized refrigerator. Two six packs of seven-ounce Rolling Rocks, a package of olive loaf, a jar of pickles and eggs. He liked things that didn't go bad. He popped the cap off a pony, finished it with four quick swallows, and opened another. Tiny beers were Taylor's concession to the possibility that his father had passed on his alcoholism. If he drank in small measures and never for breakfast, he'd be okay.

He tuned in WABC on the Emerson all-in-one stereo system. "Have You Ever Been Mellow?"

"No," he said aloud.

The song ended. "Black Water" by the Doobie Brothers followed. This Taylor liked. "Some Kind of Wonderful" by Grand Funk was next. Not really his kind of music, but he appreciated the way the band drove their sound. He opened another beer in celebration of two decent songs in a row and was immediately disappointed when the DJ announced, "A debut at number ten on the charts. Luuuuv this one. 'Get Dancin' by Disco Tex & His Sex-O-Lettes."

He switched to WNBC. Again, "Have You Ever Been Mellow?" *Shit. Why aren't they recording any good rock 'n roll anymore? Why do I sound like an old fart?*

He flicked cassettes around in the shoebox next to the stereo, pulled out Lou Reed's *Rock 'n' Roll Animal*, and polished off another Rolling Rock pony as "Sweet Jane" ended. There were four long tracks left on the live album. He allowed himself one beer per song. He pulled himself under the blankets and started to review the day but almost immediately saw Laura's eyes, her smile then her neck and curves. Who was he trying to kid? Even if he could face her, he couldn't bring her to a trailer parked in his driveway. The damn house was months from being finished. He fell asleep thinking everything in his life was on hold.

PART II:

Wednesday, March 12, 1975

4

———◆———

AN EXPLOSIVE CRASH. Taylor took the steps two at a time from the 6 train up to an overcast day at Third Avenue and 138th Street. Down toward 137th in the direction of the Deegan, flames leaped up through a roofless six-story apartment block. Fire engines poured water on one more building burning in the South Bronx. Looked like a four-alarm call. A wall collapsed, sending the flames higher. The blocks between Taylor and the fire weren't city blocks, but a waste of rubble except for one lonely three-story brownstone so far untouched. How long would that one last?

Sirens wailed in the opposite direction, to the north, where black smoke corkscrewed into the sky. The acrid smell of cooking plastic caught at the back of his throat. This happened daily, unreported by any of the newspapers, which all considered half a dozen fires too commonplace in the South Bronx. Even the *Daily News* had given up.

At a little past eight, Taylor arrived at the Graham Book Bindery. It was still standing. He was relieved and just a little amazed. The place was a relic, built when factories were temples of commerce, with an art deco facade, carved eagles on pillars standing on each side of the front door, and some sort of naked god grasping a book crowning the roof. A warehouse next door was boarded up. The lot on the other side contained nothing but broken bricks.

Inside, his optimism faded. The reception area had been ransacked. Papers carpeted the floor. A single chair lay on its side by the water-stained front wall. The Graham Book Bindery, while standing, looked like it had been abandoned.

"Hello?"

"Back here."

He followed the hall toward one lit doorway. This was a whole lot of effort to track down a missing homeless man. He didn't care. Chasing a lead on Joshua Harper was better than obit duty. Hell, working any lead was. Maybe he'd find someone was killing off homeless people. The City Desk couldn't ignore that. He stopped at the open door. A balding old man sat on a folding chair sifting through files, tossing most on the floor, putting a few in a box.

"I'm Taylor from the *Messenger-Telegram*."

"We stopped advertising ten years ago."

"I'm a reporter. I'm trying to track down a former employee."

"We have many, many of those. My brother-in-law moved everything over to Jersey City a month ago. Fired all the union men. Smart Yid, my brother-in-law. I'm packing the last of the records."

"Would you have any information on a Joshua Harper?"

"I'm not taking personnel. That's next door. Help yourself."

"What will happen to this place?"

"Did you see the neighborhood?" The man nodded his egg-shaped head at the room's single window.

"The building's going to burn? *Accidentally*?"

The old man laughed until he started wheezing. He took a puff on a thin black cigar and wheezed some more. "The smart Yid isn't paying insurance anymore. He doesn't care what happens so long as it's off his books. This place is a total loss.

Property value, zero. The South Bronx, zero."

Taylor went into the next room, which was windowless and lined on both sides with gray file cabinets. He pulled the drawer marked "H-J," and to his surprise, found "Harper, Joshua" after quickly fingering manila tabs fuzzy from use and age. Tracking someone down was like this. Either easy, or very very hard. He flipped through smeared carbons of memos that said Harper had been cautioned three times for drinking on the job and finally fired for having a bottle at his machine. The home address was 90 52nd Avenue in Queens. That was Elmhurst. Any worries he had about this trip being a waste of time vanished. Something good was going to come from following this lead.

"Thanks." Taylor stopped in the doorway. "I found a file. You certain you don't remember anything about Joshua Harper?"

"Not a thing. I'm just my brother-in-law's accountant. The dumb Yid who gets to pack the tax files. Whoever Harper was, he was lucky he got out when he did. It's time to move on. Saw it in Europe. I'll see it again. Of this, I'm sure. We've all gone to Jersey and we're not looking back." He stopped sorting. "You said you write for the newspaper."

Taylor nodded.

"I buy five newspapers every day. Four New York dailies, yours included, and *Foverts*."

"The Yiddish daily?"

"*Foverts* was the first paper I read when I got here. First paper I *could* read in America. Back then, before the war, the Bronx was the Borough of the Jews. Half here were Jews. Touch any person on the street, and it's 50-50 he's a Jew. That wasn't true *anywhere* in the Old World."

"That's not true in the Bronx anymore, either."

"Indeed. So I buy all these papers. They report the South Bronx is burning up four blocks a week. I read that twelve square miles will be destroyed by year's end. I read the city has lost almost half a million people since 1970. I don't read all this in one big article. It's in bits and pieces, sprinkled through different stories, like a puzzle I'm supposed to solve. There's no one big picture of this calamity. No one is trying to solve it."

"You're right, I'm afraid. I'm just tracking down a missing homeless man."

"I see. Bits and pieces." He shook his head and puffed on the little cigar. The gray smoke gave off a hint of cinnamon. "I'll watch the fire from Jersey City."

He went back to his files, and Taylor headed to the subway. Not far away, orange flames inside of billowing black smoke were still consuming the apartment building.

WHEN TAYLOR ARRIVED at his desk, Lou Marmelli was pissed off, his watery green eyes glaring. The obituaries editor resented typing one more word than his self-established daily quota, and the calls from the funeral homes had come in thick and fast. The arctic weather killed six old people overnight, in their homes or in hospitals. Pneumonia was the featured player. Taylor offered to handle all of them. That calmed Marmelli down enough to go downstairs to get tea, though probably that break included a stop at the City Desk to whisper a complaint in Worth's ear.

Taylor propped the Polaroid of the dead kid against an empty coffee cup and studied it. He slid it across the desk then held back for a second. He didn't want to feel stupid or crazy or both, but he couldn't help himself. He finished the trip to place the snapshot side by side with the framed picture of an Army corporal in dress uniform. His brother, Billy. The same brown hair. The resemblance ended there, though. Billy's features were handsome enough yet lacked the boy's delicacy. Billy's nose had been broken twice in Golden Gloves. His eyes were brown and fierce in the way they searched out something inside, perhaps behind, the camera lens. The boy's were empty gray in death. Taylor leaned the Polaroid back against the cup.

The Criss+Cross Directory provided a phone number for

Joshua Harper's address in Queens. A woman answered and said she and her husband bought the house from Marion Harper almost two years ago. Did she have a forwarding address? No, but she knew Marion moved to Topeka. She asked Taylor to tell the paperboy to stop trying to get them to take the *Empty*. Her husband was a *Daily News* man.

Topeka directory assistance had two Marion Harpers. The first was eighty and near deaf. The second answered on the third ring. She was Joshua Harper's wife.

"I don't want to talk to the paper. Why should I? I split with him two years ago. Leave me alone."

"I'm just trying to find him on behalf of some friends."

"Friends? What kind of joke is this? He's already been found. The police phoned yesterday. He's dead. Isn't that what you're calling about?"

"I'm sorry to hear that." Taylor straightened as his missing person search became something else.

"Are you? Why?" Her voice was hard.

"Some people here were worried about him. He'll be missed."

"You don't …." Her voice softened. "Don't get me wrong. I didn't wish him dead. I stopped crying for Joshua a long time ago. Jimmy doesn't need any more tears. Joshua kept telling me he was sick. He wasn't sick. He was weak. Ruined everything we had in New York."

"The NYPD called you?"

"No, Akron police."

"Akron?"

"They said he had a heart attack in the Greyhound station. He'd been there all night. He had no money on him and a ticket that only got him that far. He was coming out here to see us. To see Jimmy, our son. To talk to me, he said, all sozzled when he called a couple days ago. I don't know what made him head out during this awful freeze. Or maybe I do. Another one of the brilliant ideas he got on a bender. I didn't want this to happen, but I didn't want him to get here either. That was the last thing

I needed. So, in a way, maybe I wished him dead. *That's* what I've been crying about all morning. The only thing."

She hung up.

Marion Harper was the first widow he'd talked to since moving to obits. Now there was an irony. He was used to grief from the police beat. It was like listening to the same tune over and over again, while waiting for that one different riff, the piece of information that mattered. God help him, he missed everything about being a police reporter.

The Akron Police Department confirmed the death.

Taylor couldn't write an obituary for Joshua Harper; Lou Marmelli would never allow a *nobody* on his page. Death notices, on the other hand, were for everybody. More accurately, for the nobodies who didn't merit obits. Families paid fifty cents a word for classified ads printed at the bottom of the obituaries page in tiny, seven-point type.

Harper's personnel file gave Taylor enough to write the notice. He added one more line. "He leaves behind his beloved wife Marion and son James of Topeka." He put his address down for the billing department. Obit duty was making him soft. Or maybe he couldn't stand to see Harper miss his one shot at making it into the paper.

Taylor put a call into the missing persons bureau. A harried clerk said he'd "try" to call back with reports on all the teens from the past couple weeks. *Try* was the kiss of death from an NYPD clerk. He'd have to go down there and wait until he got the information he wanted. The dead boy hadn't lived on the street much more than two weeks. That he was sure of.

He spent the rest of the morning churning out one obit after another, hardly noticing what he was writing as he strung together the laundry lists the morticians read off to him. At two, he dropped the last copy in Marmelli's box and put on his jacket.

"Lunch."

"It's a lunch *hour*. Remember that."

5

————◆————

TAYLOR TOOK AN empty stool at the counter of the Odysseus Coffee Shop at Madison and 75th. The red vinyl seats still shone like new. That was his grandfather's handiwork.

"You see the Acropolis there," Grandpop explained to him once, pointing at the picture on the wall of the Oddity, the name regulars gave the coffee shop. "Place like that, wonder of the world, doesn't fall apart all at once. It's little cracks. That's what starts it crumbling. I'm not letting that happen to my restaurant. I fix the little cracks right away."

Two minutes after Taylor's arrival, his grandfather slid a cheese omelet onto the counter and filled a coffee mug.

"You look awful, Coleridge."

"Grandpop!"

"All right. Then Col. I won't call you by just a last name like we're truck drivers working together."

Grandpop, barrel-chested and wearing his year-round uniform of an apron over a white T-shirt and dungarees, stood behind the counter holding the glass coffeepot. He had a big head, big hands, and bright dark eyes. The old man claimed he always knew Taylor's order. He usually did. Taylor liked an omelet when he was at a loss for what to do next.

The aroma of omelets and coffee enticed him and he dug in. The spikey taste of onion mingled with the cheddar cheese. Just the way he liked it. He followed with the coffee and went over what he had so far. There was the unidentified dead boy, the jacket sewn with flags, and its owner, the missing Mark Voichek. Plus the late Joshua Harper. They weren't all linked, but one way or another, he had been chasing all of them at once. He walked a difficult line, trying to prove himself to Worth and Marmelli before they could fire him. He hadn't thought through how he'd work a story on the side. It was easy to forget the challenge when he was out after a lead in the Bronx. The difficulty crashed down on him after three hours of pounding out obits.

"Why are you dodging me?"

Laura Wheeler had arrived unannounced. Though angry, she was still beautiful, with thick, raven hair and dark brown eyes that snapped with emotion.

He turned on the stool. "Listen, I'm sorry. I wasn't dodging you, not really."

"Bullshit!" Her dark brown eyes flashed. "You were. Or you wouldn't be apologizing."

Two cabbies at the counter looked over.

"Hello, Laura." Grandpop moved down the counter and addressed her as if he hadn't heard a thing. "Very nice to once again see one of my grandson's colleagues at the great *New York Messenger-Telegram*. Col, show some manners. Take Laura to a table. Booth six in the corner. Very private."

"I don't think Laura wants—"

"Hello, Stamitos. I'd love lunch. Your grandson's a hard man to track down." She turned and headed in the direction of the booth.

Taylor got up and moved to take his plate and coffee cup. Grandpop waved him away. "You're not working here today. Go sit down."

Taylor slid across the bench, and Grandpop delivered his lunch. "What can I get you, Laura?"

"That omelet looks great. Tomatoes and green peppers, please."

"No cheese, Laura? American? Swiss? *Good* feta?"

"No cheese, thank you."

"Col, you want anything else?"

"I'm fine."

His grandfather left with what was supposed to be a sly backward glance.

"I've met someone who gets to use your first name." Laura sounded impressed.

"Don't get any ideas."

"You wish." She smiled, and like any smile that played across her face, it made her more stunning. "Why are you pissed at me?"

"I'm not."

"So, Roddy's right. You're pissed at *everyone*?"

"That the prevailing view in the cop shop?" He took a bite of omelet.

"Look, I figured you needed some space. All that pride. You're in a deep funk. So I gave you a month. Two months go by and you're still avoiding everyone at the paper but Worthless. Of all people! Him and that old fart who runs obits. I call and you ignore my messages. You've helped me more than anyone else at the *MT*."

"I can't help you now. I'm an obituary writer."

"You're the best goddamned reporter in the place."

The passion in her voice forced Taylor to raise his eyes from his plate. Laura's porcelain-white skin reddened delightfully at any sort of emotion—anger, embarrassment, happiness.

He didn't have a good answer. "I don't need your pity."

"No, you don't. You're wallowing in it fine all on your own. I stopped by again this morning. How can an obit writer be out of the office so much?"

"I was over in the South Bronx."

"South Bronx?"

"I've got a lead on a good story, believe it or not." He couldn't help it. He needed to talk to someone. He told her about the search for Joshua Harper and Mark Voichek, all to ID a dead kid at Bellevue. He threw in the Street Sweepers for good measure.

"Man, Taylor, I'd hate to see what you'd do if they put you on the society desk."

In spite of himself, Taylor chuckled and shook his head. "What do you want from me, Laura?"

"I'm worried about you. You're one of the smart ones in that place."

"That's not saying much."

"And to be honest," she sipped her coffee, "I need your help."

"Help?" It surprised him. He was having a hard enough time helping himself.

"They're sticking me with all the nickel-and-dime stories. Two alarms, B&Es. Half don't even make the Metro Briefs. Worse, they've got me doing research for other reporters. You know why? Because I'm a woman. Merton is covering a multiple on the Upper West Side. He *just* got out of grad school. Even I've been there longer."

"He doesn't know what he's doing."

"He's a man. That's all he needs. I talked with Kathy Loring on the political desk. Unless I want to work the society beat, *girls* end up doing research at the mighty *MT,* beacon of reform and liberality."

Grandpop set Laura's plate and coffee down. She took a bite and smiled. "Mmm, that's so good, Stamitos. Your food *is* amazing." Her cheeks tinged pink. "My plan is to uncover my own leads. I want your help."

"Welcome to the find-your-own-story club."

Grandpop topped off their coffee cups. He was visiting the table at least twice as often as necessary. He squeezed Taylor's shoulder as he went back to the counter.

"I like your grandfather."

"Such an old dear."

"I don't mean it that way. He cares about you. It's obvious."

"He's the best my family has. Left, that is."

"Your family did pretty well by you."

He stabbed a couple of fries and a piece of his omelet. He *so* missed talking to Laura. Was she interested in him or his story ideas? He had never been sure. Christ, trying to figure out what a woman wanted turned him into a complete idiot. Everyone seemed to be playing by a different rulebook. The younger women, certainly. The sexual revolution and all that. The ones in their thirties, like him? They'd settled down long ago with other men after adding up the hours and pay of a newspaperman.

The silence opened between them. Two months ago, they'd talked all the time about crimes, stories, and competitors. What to bring up? Taylor would die before he'd talk about writing obits.

"I watched *Dragnet* last night." Laura smiled. "It made me think of you."

"How's that?"

"Joe Friday is always saying that thing, 'Just the facts, ma'am.'"

"That's very funny."

"I'm not trying to be funny. That's you. You always say it's about the facts, always about the facts."

"'Facts are stubborn things. Whatever may be our wishes, our inclinations, or the dictates of our passion, they cannot alter the state of facts.' John Adams."

"You don't usually throw quotes around. That's Worth's habit."

"Okay, that hurt." He clutched his heart in mock pain. "There's only a couple I've liked enough to memorize. I do get the facts. Enough of them and I know what happened. Then I write the story."

"You still trying to find the girl?"

"Yes."

"You got the facts on her. It was an incredible story."

Taylor stared at her. "You know it was a fraud." Gloom dropped over him. It was as if the mistake followed him around, waiting for someone to bring it up.

"No. You said the cop who introduced you to the little girl was a fraud. The girl wasn't."

"I can't prove it."

"You watched her mother jab a needle into her skinny arm. I can see it like I was there. You wrote it that well."

"Everyone believes I invented the whole damn thing."

"I believe you." A simple declarative sentence followed by a simple declarative smile. "I'll help. If you find Tinker Bell, everyone believes your story. You're back on cops. I can do a lot of reporting while pulling files for the *boys* at the *MT*."

"All right. Since we're both looking for stories, come with me." Taylor got up, determined to move rather than wallow. He stopped at the gray cash register. "I'll pay for both, Grandpop."

"No you won't." Laura pulled a big wallet out of her bag.

"No you won't," echoed Grandpop. "Nobody pays. Family guests never pay."

"But Stamitos—"

"No buts. Go make the city safe for truth and democracy."

"I wouldn't argue with him." Taylor put his wallet away. "No one ever wins."

"Not even you?"

"Definitely not me."

They headed for the door.

"I'd pay to see that."

"Save your money." Taylor pulled open the door and the bell jingled.

"For what?"

"Buy me a drink."

"You let girls buy you drinks?"

"Nope, only women."

"Let me think of a place. Tomorrow night work?"

"It does."

6

———◆———

In Duffy Square, Taylor and Laura stopped in front of the statue of Jimmy Cagney. Really it was George M. Cohan. That was the problem with fiction. It cast a shadow over reality. The whores and pimps of the night before were gone, replaced by three-card Monte teams, yelling and waving hands so violently Taylor was sure they weren't working marks yet. Each team's lookout lounged half a block away in such obvious fashion it was clear the biggest surprise to any of them would be actual cops coming to bust up the games. The barkers for the sex shows had been replaced by the day shift. Same clothes, same gestures, same patter. A string of scruffy students lined up at the TKTS booth for half-price Broadway shows.

Taylor leaned his shoulder against the statue's rough granite plinth and looked across the intersection of Broadway and Seventh Avenue. Here was the "X" that marked the Crossroads of the World. A low gray ceiling swirled above. A front was coming down from the Great Lakes. Snow was in the air, the wet odor of a lot of snow. The temperature had moved up to 20, balmy if it weren't for the damp. Laura hugged her black parka tighter, and people hurried by with their heads down.

The chill from the granite seeped through the layers of Taylor's clothing into his shoulders until he had to straighten up to escape the ache.

"Who are we waiting for?" Laura asked.

"A source of mine. A leader of the homeless of sorts."

"That story you did? About the homeless guy who was beat to death. You quoted a guy named Harry Jansen."

"Good memory."

"Your stories stick."

He turned to see if she was joking. The Nanook-of-the-North coat hid her curves. Another curse of the extended winter. Inside the tube hood, her mouth was drawn in a serious line. He was wrong. He didn't know how to deal with her on this basis. Kidding around always made everything easier. Less risky.

"Here he comes."

Harry Jansen crossed from the west side of Broadway. He wore a poncho that flapped up in the wind like black wings.

"This is Laura Wheeler, a colleague at the paper."

"A pleasure, Miss Wheeler. Or is it Miz?"

"It's Miz, or I'd like it to be. The newspaper business is pretty old-fashioned. Call me Laura."

"Hello, Laura. It remains a pleasure." Jansen looked at the statue. "I'm mighty glad I'm living, that's all." He patted the base. "It's from one of his songs. No one remembers it now. 'Yankee Doodle Dandy,' 'Give My Regards to Broadway,' 'Over There.' Those people recall. The upbeat, patriotic ones. Never, 'I'm Mighty Glad I'm Living, That's All.' I wonder why?"

Laura looked at Taylor.

He wasn't even going to try for an explanation. "Have you had any more trouble at the shelter?"

"None. Maybe you scared off the Street Sweepers for good."

"I hope so. I'm afraid I've got bad news."

"Joshua? He's dead, isn't he?"

"Yes. I'm sorry."

"How?"

"Had a heart attack outside the Akron bus station."

"This is terrible." Jansen's voice lost the electric charge that made him sound like a gypsy prince. "Seven dead in two weeks for the want of simple shelter."

"I don't think that's the case with Joshua. The Akron police said it was his heart. He was trying to get to his wife and kid and ran out of money. Maybe he was drinking?"

"I don't see how it's any different. What's happening to the body?"

"I don't know. It's up to the Akron cops." Taylor understood Jansen's anger. The man felt responsibility for his transient tribe. Some didn't want help. Some didn't know they needed it. An impossible job, and all the while Jansen was trying to keep himself alive.

"His wife isn't doing anything?"

"I doubt it. She's finished."

"Then we will. We'll go get him."

"You can't move the body. Only an undertaker can."

"Get us one. Get us an undertaker to move the body. We'll give him a funeral here where his home was."

"Do you know what that will cost?"

"We'll get the money." Jansen pulled the black poncho tight. "Please, just make the arrangements. You know all those wonderful people in the death business. Set it up. We're not leaving Joshua in Akron."

"All right. I'll make some calls."

"This is such a bad business. Our people are dying out here. What about the boy at Bellevue? Do you still think his death is suspicious?"

"He wasn't homeless, but I won't know why he was found in Voichek's field jacket until I talk to Voichek."

"The news there isn't good either. I just don't know how bad it is. Voichek's certainly in trouble. He's moving around the city, fast, never stopping long. Torres the Kid saw him about eight hours ago rushing through Port Authority."

"Leaving town?"

"Torres the Kid thought so. Until Voichek hustled out back past the buses and kept on going. The Kid tried to follow. Voichek got furious. That's not like him, particularly with the Kid. He screamed at the boy. Said everybody must stay away. Someone is after him."

"Who's Torres?"

"One of ours. Been on the street about two years. He's thirteen, maybe fourteen. Voichek was teaching him how to survive."

Laura stepped in a little closer as the wind picked up. "Did the two of them have a relationship?"

"No! Voichek looked after Torres. That was it. He's not into boys. Not at all. Torres' father beat him something terrible. He moved out with nowhere to go. We don't allow abuse."

"You're doing a lot better than the city shelters," Laura said.

"That's why they have empty beds when it's freezing cold. It's fear, not madness, that puts people on steam grates."

Taylor pulled out his notebook and flipped it open. "If Voichek is on the run, how do we find him?"

"Everybody's looking. I've got all the vets walking the Manhattan grid like they're scouting the Mekong." Jansen lit a cigarette with a silver lighter, inhaled deep and blew out. The blue cloud's tobacco scent somehow made Taylor a little warmer in the frigid air. "We *will* find Voichek. Whatever he's up against, he'll get our help. I'll call when I have news."

He stepped off the curb and walked west. Two sailors in Navy pea coats and dress-white bellbottoms crossed the other way. Each had a good-looking young woman on his arm. They were all laughing. Laura nodded at the four. "Some things don't change."

"Yeah, but they're the exception now. Grandpop used to bring me here when I was a kid. My God, the place was crowded. Families, teenagers, service men, old couples, tourists. Everyone was dressed to the nines. And the lights. Neon in every color. News zippers slipping headlines around buildings. Nothing was more amazing than that Bond sign." He pointed four stories up at the word *Bond,* which was all that remained. "It stretched the entire block. A giant man and woman, and between them, a waterfall four stories high. A real goddamn waterfall in the sky. The signs here were like Broadway productions. They changed them to keep everyone's attention. Now they don't even bother to turn the lights on."

"I thought that was because of the energy crisis."

"Times Square should be exempt. The world looks at this place."

"Not anymore."

"Maybe not, but giving up is half the reason why."

They crossed to the west side of Broadway. The clock centered in the "O" of *Bond* said it was already past three-thirty. Marmelli was going to be furious. Again. Taylor couldn't tell if he was going two steps forward and one step back or the other way around. Was he fighting to win back his old job or getting himself fired from the awful one he had?

Laura turned to him. "Does it really matter to you whether Harper's body gets home?"

"I said I'd do it."

"Does it matter?"

"It matters to Jansen."

"I want to know what you care about. You're arranging a funeral for a homeless man. I think that's pretty amazing."

"Hardly." He waved her off. "I need Jansen's help."

"I know. 'Facts are stubborn things. And whatever may be our wishes—' "

"Now you're getting it." He smiled. "I should get back to the paper before Marmelli has kittens. You know everything about what I'm working on. Want to help?"

"Definitely. I'll call when I get back. I've got to pick up some court documents for the boys."

Her snorkel hood was down. She smiled and her beauty warmed him. He'd been an idiot to avoid her. He wanted to tell Laura but didn't know how to admit the mistake without making it worse.

She squeezed his forearm and started walking down Broadway. "I'll find a good place for us to go tomorrow night."

The words slipped around One Times Square on the sole remaining news ticker:

NORTH VIETNAMESE MARCH SOUTH
THROUGH CENTRAL HIGHLANDS ...
CONSTRUCTION STARTS ON ALASKA
PIPEPLINE ... MARINER 10 HEADS BACK
TOWARD MERCURY ...

For the first time in weeks, he could look forward to an evening out. He couldn't leave it be, though. What if Laura chose somewhere he didn't fit in? What if he came off as old-fashioned or just plain old? He shook his head at his insecurities and took the stairs down to the subway.

7

---◆---

As SOON AS Taylor was at his desk, Marmelli came over. "I will not have you disappearing for an entire afternoon."

"It was lunch."

"I'm telling you. This is your last warning." His voice was pitched so high it had to be annoying the little dogs on Park Avenue. "I'll go to Garfield and Worth. I didn't want to take you in the first place."

Taylor's phone rang, and he held up his hand. "Sorry, Lou, probably a funeral home." He grabbed the receiver. He welcomed a mortician at this point.

"I've missed your work, Taylor." A familiar lisp. "You know what a fan I am."

"Pickwick?"

"Did you miss me?"

"Didn't expect to hear from you." He lowered his voice. Marmelli returned to his desk and continued to watch. "What, you need an obit now?"

"Oh ye of little faith. How can you be so cruel to your very best source?"

"You're not a source. I *know* all my sources. You're an

anonymous tipster who for some reason enjoys using me."

"You have struck your Pickwick in his heart. Would you prefer to meet in a parking garage? Give me a disgusting pornographic nickname? Deep Throat. Disgusting. Have I not been the *source* of some excellent scoops for you and your *Empty*?"

"You also sent me all over Staten Island looking for a gambling ring fronted by church bingo nights."

Pickwick giggled like a TV comedian. It wasn't funny to Taylor. His anger rose. He'd spent two weeks traipsing the wilderness of New York's most outer borough before Pickwick admitted there was no ring.

"Oh, I'm sorry, Taylor." Pickwick snickered again. "That was a good one. I told you why I did that. I need to protect my situation here. If I throw in a smelly red herring or two, the people who watch you won't be led back to me. You see that, don't you? We must have some false scents to keep the hounds at bay. What about all the other stories?"

Marmelli took a call. *Thank God.* Taylor faced away from his desk to put his back to the obit editor. "Yeah, sure. I got a couple leads."

Actually, five stories had panned out. The one about a con artist who worked for the Brooklyn bunko squad was the best of them, though the drug ring in a midtown pharmacy got good play too. Taylor could no more ignore Pickwick's anonymous tips than he could walk past a four-alarm blaze. He was certain of one thing. The man worked somewhere in the system that gave him visibility into what the police were doing and the crimes they were missing.

"You do joke. You're wasted on obits, you know. I can't even tell which are yours. Do they force all of you to write in the same morbid style?"

"Did you call to insult me? I've got a whole newsroom full of people to do that."

"I've decided your banishment has gone on long enough. Such an awful sentence."

"Do you know who set me up?"

"Not yet. I'm working on it."

"Did you set me up?"

"Well, I'd know already if it was me, wouldn't I? I don't act. I've told you. I watch and I write my papers. I tell you *some* of what I see."

"What do you know about Tinker Bell?"

"At this point, only what I read in your rapidly retracted article. You're right, though. Someone set you up. The big problem is figuring out who. You've pissed off so very many people, inside the police department and out of it. Tell me now. You're looking for a teenage boy at missing persons?"

That didn't surprise Taylor. It wasn't the first time Pickwick had already known what Taylor was working on. "There's a dead teenager at Bellevue. He's dressed to look homeless, but I don't think he is."

"Yes, I know. Two families on the Upper East Side are missing boys similar in age and description to your corpse. All reported in the past two weeks."

"What about other neighborhoods?"

"Nothing even close. There was a boy on the Westside, but he came home last night."

"Pickwick, if this is another—"

"You'll still follow my leads."

There was nothing to do but write down the addresses as Pickwick rattled them off.

8

———◆———

DEEP IN WINTER darkness, the streets of the Upper East Side were still busy as the well-bred, moneyed set jumped out of cabs and private cars and headed for the warmth of luxury living. Taylor arrived at the first address, a townhouse in Yorkville. All the lights were on, a seemingly warm invitation in the aching cold. Men and women were silhouetted against the windows.

At the door, a gray-haired man said the missing seventeen-year-old had been dug out of a drift on the thruway two days ago. The family was holding the wake. "Why are you bothering us now?"

"Vulture," said a younger man, who stepped forward and pushed Taylor in the chest. "Vulture!"

Taylor backed down the steps to the sidewalk.

"I'm sorry. I'm trying to identify someone. Similar age and build. My mistake. You have my condolences."

"I'm calling the cops," said the older man. "Taylor, right? *The Empty*? You have no right harassing the grieving."

Yeah, and I'll be the one writing your son's obit in the morning.
He shoved his leather-gloved hands into the field jacket,

repeatedly looking over his shoulder for a bus to hop to get to the second address. His legs were losing their bravado. No buses came, and he walked all the way to the heavy oak door and polished brass knocker of a four-story, redbrick townhouse on 69th off First Avenue. More than one floor in Manhattan meant money. Four said these folks swam in the stuff. If you pissed them off, your publisher got the phone call. Then he'd learn his fate a whole lot sooner than Tuesday. He'd never once gotten a story by worrying. Now wasn't the time to start. He rapped the knocker three times; the metallic crack echoed inside the house.

A good-looking brunette in a little black dress, the kind for something formal, answered the door.

"I'm Taylor with the *Messenger-Telegram*. I'd like to—"

"My husband's out." She swayed as if she heard music. Warm air from the house blew out a hint of expensive perfume. "We were at a dinner, and the men needed to talk. They always need to talk. You'll have to get him tomorrow."

"I can talk to you about this."

"Oh I don't talk about legal business." She was ready to swing the door shut in his face.

"Legal business?"

"What else? He's the assistant corporation counsel for New York. Big whoopty doo!" She wobbled on pointed, three-inch heels.

"I wasn't aware."

"You must be aware of Johnny Scudetto."

"The Democratic boss for New York County?"

"Give the man a prize. Big Johnny is certainly the boss. And my father. Him I *never* talk about. City business I *never* talk about." She leaned out toward him and brought with her the juniper and lemon of gin and tonic. She acted like she'd had more than one. "Bad for the girls to talk about any of it. So don't play like you don't know who we are."

"I don't cover politics. I'm following up a missing person report."

"Declan?"

"You're Lydia McNally?"

She swung the door wide and the plaything look fled her face. "Oh God, I'm worried sick. Do you have information?"

"May I come in?"

"Yes, please. This way."

Lydia McNally walked down the hallway, showing off her slender, bare back and long, tapered legs. The view made him wish the hallway was a block long. The slight wobble from the alcohol and the high heels only made the show that much better. Declan McNally's mother probably wasn't too drunk to know the effect she was having. She turned off the hall into the living room and settled into the kind of brown leather chair you usually found in a private club. Another, similar chair stood opposite. She motioned to it, picked up a clinking glass and took a sip.

"Do you want something to drink?"

If you don't drink on the job, you're not a drunk. "I'm fine. Thanks. What was the dinner this evening?"

"You said you're here about Declan."

Lydia McNally's features were those of a beautiful Italian peasant girl somewhere in her ancestry. Thick brown hair, darker eyes and voluptuous lips.

"No, I said I'm here about *a* missing boy."

"Declan's been gone since Sunday night. Four days!" She rubbed her temples, and it was as if a shadow fell across her face. "The police have been fucking useless. My other son's a cop. My husband *was* a cop. Still they've turned up nothing. Declan's doing this to piss us off. Fine, I dig that. Somebody must have laid eyes on him."

"When exactly did you see him last?"

"At about eight that evening. He had an argument with his father."

"Over what?"

"The usual teenage shit. Yelling about homework. I walked in right after Declan stormed out. Con waited up till four. Next morning we started calling the other kids. His friends know where he is. I'm sure of it. They claimed they don't. The little shits. He's staying with one of them, and the kids are all lying about it. The maids won't say a thing. The parents don't even know what's going on in their own homes."

"Does he fight with your husband a lot?"

"He fights with everyone a lot. Me. Con. His teachers. He's smart. Too smart for his own damn good. He gets this look. I swear it's just like my father, like when Big Johnny is really playing political mind games with someone. That's the hard part for Con. He can't fight with my dad. So it all comes out with Declan."

The fireplace mantle was crowded with pictures, but Taylor couldn't see them from the chair. He wanted to be sure before showing her the photo.

"Think I'll have a beer now, if that's okay."

"The housekeeper's off. Please help yourself. The kitchen's the second door down the hall."

He passed half a dozen pictures with the boy at the morgue in them. Different ages, same face. Excitement mingled with a hint of fear. The adrenal charge that came from knowing very bad news before anyone else in the world. He was on dangerous ground. Lydia McNally couldn't think he kept digging for information after he was sure the boy was Declan. He came back into the room with the beer, took a swallow and set it in an ashtray on a side table.

"Mrs. McNally, I need you to look at a picture." He got up and slipped the Polaroid out of his pocket.

"Declan?"

"I'm very sorry. This was taken at Bellevue. If this is your son—"

"Oh, God. No no. Of course it's him." Tears welled and

she started crying. She gasped to get the words out. "What happened?"

"It appears he froze to death in Gansevoort Market."

"Froze to death? In Gansevoort Market?" Spoken like the strangest possible combination of words. Words she couldn't make meaning out of in that particular order. She gave out a sound that wasn't a word, more like a groan, fell back into the chair and sobbed. After a few minutes, the sobs turned into a quiet sort of moaning.

"Is there someone I can call?"

She looked up as though surprised he was still there, made to lift herself out of the chair but couldn't. "Pour me a drink."

He got the bottle, opened it and tipped.

"More gin. More goddamned gin!" He added two fingers of tonic. "Now too much. You're no goddamned help if you can't do it right." The front door opened and closed. She started yelling. "Con! Constable get in here."

Constable McNally walked into the room, sized up the scene and tilted his head to the side. A surprised look on his handsome Irish face, the kind you saw all the time in New York, with clear blue eyes, pale skin and the faded hints of a freckled childhood. His hand went to his back, where an ex-cop would carry his gun, and he spoke in a cold, level voice. "What's going on?"

"I'm Taylor from the *Messenger-Telegram*."

"The paper? We don't allow press in the house. Lydia, what's he doing in here?" He advanced on Taylor.

"No, honey. It's Declan." She reached her hands out to him. "It's Declan."

"Mr. McNally, I'm sorry." Taylor handed him the picture. "I have very bad news for you. I came to your house to identify a boy who's died."

"Declan." A statement, not a question. "Declan." He dropped into the empty leather chair and put his face in his hands.

Lydia McNally forced herself to her feet, started toward him but shuddered twice and puked onto the blue and white Dutch tile in front of the fireplace. The sound made Taylor's stomach lurch. She looked up from the mess, reached her hand to wipe her mouth and toppled over sideways. Taylor, still standing after pouring the drink, reached her before she cracked her head on a marble-topped coffee table and cradled the mother's head and shoulders.

Constable McNally came over and took Taylor's place. "Oh shit, she's unconscious. Call an ambulance."

There was a black phone on a side table, but Taylor decided to give the couple privacy and used a wall phone in the kitchen. He told the 911 operator the address and waited there for a few minutes.

McNally still sat on the living room floor holding his wife's head in his lap. Her eyes were closed. His face was pitched between grief and concern. It was time to leave. They didn't need more questions now. He couldn't answer them anyway.

McNally looked up. "How did you find my son?"

"He came in to Bellevue as a John Doe. He was found on the street in the Gansevoort."

"Oh God." He shook his head slowly. "You know this and the police don't?"

"He's being treated as a homeless person. Five others have died of exposure in the past few weeks. I thought something was wrong. He didn't look like he'd been on the street. Though he was dressed to make you think he was."

"What did he have on?" McNally's cop instincts must be kicking in even in the midst of grief. Asking questions could get you to focus beyond the pain. He'd done it himself. A crime was easier to deal with as a problem to solve rather than something happening *to* you.

"Patched jeans, a sweater and a very distinctive Army field jacket. The jacket was owned by a homeless man named Mark Voichek."

"Any leads on him?"

"I'm trying to track him down."

"I don't understand any of this. Declan had a temper, but how did this happen to him? We thought he was hiding out with a friend. You know, being dramatic."

"Your wife said you argued about homework."

"Yes. Hardly a big deal. He blew up and left the house."

Declan's fury meant something, and Taylor wasn't getting all of it.

Ambulance lights strobed the hallway. Taylor went outside and Lydia McNally was put in the white Cadillac wagon. Constable stepped in behind her, turned and looked at Taylor one more time then disappeared. The ambulance pulled away. This one wasn't going to Bellevue.

He walked west toward the 6 train. He didn't enjoy this part of the job. He was the one who brought grief into that house, dividing the life they had from one they couldn't imagine facing. You had to say someone was dead for them to really die. Until then, there was always hope.

PART III:
Thursday, March 13, 1975

9

———◆———

THE MORNING FLEW by, despite the pulsing headache left behind by too many little beers the night before. At noon, he set a personal record with the obit of a retired Madison Avenue executive. Twenty-one minutes from phone call to finished copy. Writing fast made anything exciting. Almost anything.

He needed the beers when he got to Queens to put out the fury burning in him. The night editor refused to put a rewrite man on the death of Declan McNally. He said he couldn't take a story from Taylor over the phone; he needed to confirm it with the cops. Anyway, Taylor wasn't allowed a byline. All "per Mr. Worth." The other papers were going to beat the *MT* on the death of Declan McNally because Worthless was such a goddamn idiot.

He dropped the ad executive's obit in Marmelli's inbox and returned to his desk.

Maybe the whole damn paper was falling apart. Was he holding onto something already lost? Ten New York newspapers had gone belly up since he started working as a copyboy. Laura's complaints yesterday about her treatment bothered him too. Was it really that bad? Women's lib meant nothing on the police beat. None of the movements of the past twenty years did, so he didn't follow them much. The civil rights campaigns produced protests and arrests, and some of the anti-war demonstrations led to riots, but he spent his time among people who needed to be liberated from addiction, poverty, and ignorance. Most crimes were committed by people trapped by bad circumstances. The victims were trapped by the very same bad circumstances. Political movements didn't break that cycle. If anything, things had gotten worse. He'd ask Laura more about the situation for women at the *MT*. He also wanted to tell her about identifying the body as Declan McNally. He missed having her desk next to his. That was something else he lost when they booted him from the police beat. First, a quick call.

A slow-speaking voice with a stutter answered the pay phone number.

"Is Jansen around?"

"Who's a-a-asking?"

"Taylor."

"No."

"Then why'd you ask my name?"

"It's what he t-t-old me to do."

"Tell him to call. I have news about Joshua's funeral arrangements."

He badly needed word from Jansen on Voichek's whereabouts. The homeless man was his best lead. And one no other reporter had. The Army jacket with the flags was going to reveal something about how Declan McNally died. Taylor was certain of it. The argument last evening with the night editor made him want the story more than any he could remember in a long time. He may have calmed the fury but he now worked at a dark, low boil.

He walked the long way around the edge of the newsroom, skirting past Society and Arts. Boisterous laughter came from the Toy Department (aka Sports). He didn't feel like taking the shorter path through the middle of the newsroom and meeting the dark stares of everyone who felt personally wounded by his story on a nine-year-old heroin addict called Tinker Bell. The week after its retraction, the puzzle editor cornered him to express his anger with a quote from Shakespeare. Taylor didn't understand the quote but guessed it was something about betrayal. Most people were less subtle.

He arrived at the small cluster of desks reserved for the cop shop. Laura wasn't at hers. He turned to go.

"You don't say hello any more," said Jack Fahey.

He turned. "Hi, Fahey. You seen Laura?"

"She's out on a story. Can't imagine what it is, though. She's supposed to be doing my research."

"I hear she's spending a lot of time doing everyone else's work."

"You don't like how we're using our cub reporters?"

Taylor held his hands up in a feigned no-argument-here gesture. "Hey, I think the *MT* should make the best use of *all* its reporters."

He leaned back on Laura's desk and caught a lingering hint of her perfume. He'd so much rather be talking to her than this asshole. Fahey sat at Taylor's old spot. That was an insult all by itself.

"Did Marmelli assign you to ID the dead kid in the morgue?" Fahey, a small man with a narrow head, compensated by talking big and writing bigger. "Everybody's going on and on about this major scoop from obits. Sorry, got that wrong. Would have been a scoop had a reporter gotten it and the paper run it."

"I had a hunch."

"A Taylor hunch? They're the best. You didn't make this McNally kid up, did you?" He snickered.

"Yeah, it's a big laugh. The grandson of the Democratic Party chief lies dead at Bellevue, and it takes an obit writer to figure *that* out. Embarrassing for the hot-shit boys in the cop shop."

"Not at all, not at all. They assigned me the McNally story. Great one, by the way. Thanks for the legwork. And you're *still* doing obits. Though there's been a lot of talk about you around the City Desk this morning. I think you may have wandered too far out of your playpen for the last time." Fahey leered as Laura walked up. "Here's your protégée now."

Taylor couldn't take anymore. He grabbed Fahey's nubby blue knit tie and pulled him out of the chair.

"Jesus, Taylor, that's all you need to do." Laura stepped in between the two men, put one hand on Taylor's hand and the other on his shoulder and exerted a gentle pressure. He let go of the tie but suddenly didn't want to lose contact with her. She moved away from him.

"You're a goddamned maniac." Fahey straightened the knot. "I thought you'd lost your mind with that fucking Tinker Bell story. Now I'm sure of it. You're a menace."

Laura's phone rang. She spoke briefly, hung up and addressed Taylor. "That was Worth. He's with Marmelli. They want to see you in the conference room."

She pointed in the general direction of the City Desk, though the cluttered newsroom layout meant she was actually pointing at a coat rack in front of a file cabinet.

"Ah shit, not those two." Taylor turned to leave what was once his favorite place at the *MT*. In the world, really.

"Take care," Laura said. "You've embarrassed them."

"Care is the last thing I'll use with those assholes."

"Goodbye, Taylor." Fahey spoke with a theatrical finality.

"Don't count on it."

Taylor entered the room used by the editors for the twice-daily Page One meetings. "You didn't need to call a meeting just to thank me."

Famous front pages—world wars ending, men walking on the moon—hung in frames from the wood-paneled walls. Red blotches discolored Marmelli's puffy face. Either he was really angry or having some kind of allergic reaction. The Barbasol smell was suffocating, as if he'd dumped a bucket of the stuff on himself that morning.

Worth pursed his lips like a schoolmarm and licked them once. "The last thing you want to do is treat this as a joke."

"Of course it's not a goddamned joke." Taylor's voice rose. "Not when Big Johnny's grandson was in Bellevue's icebox. Unidentified. Heading to a pauper's grave."

"I don't want to hear any of your self-aggrandizing." Worth tapped his finger on a sheet of paper. "The boy would've been identified eventually."

"Tell that to his parents."

"Plain and simple, you were insubordinate. You pursued something you had no business—"

"Bullshit. I brought you a good story. You could have been first with it. If your night editor weren't scared shitless of *your* goddamned shadow. It's a big story. An important New York family. This isn't about me. This is about this *news*-paper. You're supposed to give a shit about the news." He imagined the writers of the stories on the wall disgusted at hearing this conversation. What would they think of his actions? Of his attempts to set things right? The huge headlines telling of disasters and assassinations and invasions stretched upwards. Or was he shrinking?

"Nothing you did was appropriate. Going after the story. Neglecting your duties in obituaries. You're making this so very easy for me. I have a memo I'll read."

Taylor knew what that meant. He stood up. "I'm sick."

"What?"

"I said I'm sick. It's in the Guild contract. You can't take administrative action when I'm out sick."

"You're standing right here."

"Feeling terrible. This is now a sick day."

Worth looked at Marmelli. "Does the contract really say that?"

"I don't know. Papa always took care of union issues."

"Jesus H. Christ."

Taylor left the room, went quickly to his desk, grabbed his coat and notebook and walked straight across the newsroom to the elevators. He didn't give a damn about the stares now. He asked for the lobby in a loud voice. Once there, he slipped into the stairwell and climbed to the fifth floor, home of the Actuarial Department of the New Haven Life Insurance Company. He crossed the floor filled with desks in perfect rows. They took up the same space as the newsroom upstairs, but actuaries were neat and tidy people.

Down a hallway off the main floor, he entered a small room lined with file cabinets. The odor of old newsprint hung in the dry air. At a desk in the back, peering with a magnifying glass at a piece of paper under her desk lamp, sat Mrs. Wiggins. The file cabinets all around her contained brown envelopes filled with newspaper clippings filed by subject and cross-indexed, stories published during the past 118 years, all the way back to the original *New York Telegram*'s founding by Cyrus Garfield in 1857. This was the newspaper's morgue.

Mrs. Wiggins looked up. "Why hello, Taylor. I never see you anymore."

"I'm out sick today."

"You look healthy to me."

"Worth's trying to fire me."

"Ah. He was an unfortunate choice for city editor."

"No kidding."

Mrs. Wiggins, more than twice his age, shook her head. "I was sick for a couple of days right after the Korean War. When I returned, the *Telegram*'s morgue looked like vandals had ransacked it. Never again." She had high cheekbones and the curious eyes of the best sort of journalist. Fifty-five years of notating and filing newspaper articles made her a living index and an amazing resource.

"Can I use the phone?"

"Be my guest."

Taylor sat at the single study carrel in the cramped room, looked at the receiver and rapped a pencil against the desktop. He needed a plan. This was an odd sort of liberation. Worthless would find a way to get to him. It probably wouldn't take long. Until then, Taylor could do the one thing he did well. Go after the story. He should have gone out sick sooner. The best place to start was Declan McNally's obituary. He dialed the coroner's office at Bellevue.

"Which funeral home is picking up Declan McNally?"

"Be careful what you write." The clerk laughed quietly. "That body caused one holy shit storm here."

"Tell me."

"The docs got an urgent call early this morning. This unidentified body is some mucky-muck's kid. You've never seen them jump around so much." He laughed again. "They've got to get the autopsy done by tonight so Carter & Carter up in Yorkville can pick it up."

"Who's cutting?"

"Quirk."

"What time?"

"I thought you wanted to know about the funeral home."

"You've intrigued me."

"Well, I don't need to go intriguing no newspaper reporter. You've got the name of the home."

More Bellevue customer service. No matter. It was enough. He called the funeral home next. "I understand you're handling arrangements for Declan McNally. I wanted to get the information."

"This is a little irregular," said the tired voice. "Usually we call the obituaries into the papers."

"With a *prominent* family, we like to get to work right away so we can do the very best write-up."

"The family only called this morning. I don't have everything. I'll give you what I have."

An obituary, for once, became Taylor's ally. He typed up the information as it was read off. Declan Sean McNally died March 10. Son of Associate Corporation Counsel Constable McNally and Lydia (Scudetto) McNally, brother of Liam McNally of the NYPD, grandson of New York County Democratic Party Chairman John Scudetto and Maria (Carmello) Scudetto and the late Sergeant Patrick McNally of the NYPD and Mary (Murphy) McNally. The deceased was a junior at Eli Prep, on the headmaster's list since freshman year, a starter on the lacrosse team and editor of the yearbook. Calling hours at Carter & Carter Funeral Home at 346 W. 87th Street were set for tomorrow evening, with a Mass of Christian Burial at St. Patrick's Cathedral the day following.

"The cathedral?"

"You are getting *all* this, right?" The voice listed aunts, uncles and cousins and gave the details for a memorial service planned at Eli Prep for the following week.

He hung up and put a carbon of the typed notes in an interoffice envelope to Marmelli. That would surprise him. Taylor may have stretched the truth to get the info, but he didn't want to break it.

"I'm going to need some of your magic." He turned around and faced Mrs. Wiggins' desk in the back. "Everything you've got on Big Johnny Scudetto and Constable McNally. McNally is Scudetto's son-in-law. Also, Constable's wife, Lydia. And their sons Declan and Liam. I don't expect much on the boys, but it never hurts to check."

"You're still reporting?"

"Till they drag me out of here."

"What are you looking for?"

"Don't know yet."

The big stack was clips on Scudetto. No surprise. Big Johnny had been part of the Democratic machine for decades. A lot of enemies there. He pushed the pile off to the side to tackle at night, when there was no one awake to interview. By comparison, the son-in-law hadn't made much of a mark. The item on his appointment to the city job gave an interesting scrap. McNally was the attorney responsible for bids and contracts. He'd handled the legal end of millions of dollars of city purchases, from typewriter ribbons to blacktop. You could piss people off in that position too.

His first stop today would be Declan's high school before the rest of the press descended. He called Laura.

"Taylor! Christ, Worthless is trying to fire you."

"That he is. You know Eli Prep?"

"Of course."

"Is that the one you went to?"

"Just because it's a private school on the Eastside doesn't mean—"

"Please, I don't have time."

"No, I went to Dalton."

"You know Eli?"

"Well enough."

"Good. You're coming with me. Declan McNally went there and I'm going to need help talking to those kids."

"They're not going to speak Latin."

"Latin, pig Latin, it'll all be Greek to me. I want someone who can read them. Meet me at the stairs to the uptown 6."

10

———— ◆ ————

Taylor and Laura walked west on 99th Street into an icy wind. As they reached Fifth Avenue, he held up his hand, turned downtown and walked in the wrong direction like he meant to go that way.

"What is it?"

"Two detectives coming out of Eli. Demarco and Simone."

They went around the block once. Taylor checked to make sure the unmarked Ford sedan was gone before approaching the iron gates of the private school.

"These kids are going to be upset," Laura said.

"They won't be surprised to see us. Their families move and shake this city. Everything they do is news. A death in their midst ...."

"That's cynical."

"We'll see."

They went through the half-opened gates, across a cobbled driveway to an archway with the school name carved into stone, and entered the granite building.

Taylor held the door for her. "We can't go into classrooms. I was thinking his activities. Yearbook and lacrosse."

Laura checked her watch. "Classes don't end for another twenty minutes, so no winter practice yet."

Taylor gave her a look.

"I called ahead to check the schedule. I'd say the yearbook office."

"Office?"

"My yearbook had an office. A nice one."

"*MT's* newsroom must have been some come-down for you."

She spread her arms. "Money makes this world go around."

"I've told you. Greek to me."

A girl and two boys sat at a circular table in the yearbook office. The front wall was covered with black and white proof sheets. Layout tables, identical to the professional ones in the *MT's* production shop, lined the back of the room. The three kids talked in hushed near-whispers and went silent when Taylor and Laura entered.

The girl, a brunette with the figure of a woman, sniffled and gripped the cuff of her navy sweater with her fingers to wipe away tears. "You're here about Dec."

"I'm very sorry about what's happened. I'm Taylor from the *Messenger-Telegram.* This is Laura Wheeler."

"The cops just left."

One of the two boys wore a red-and-yellow-striped tie and a blue tweed blazer with a school patch stitched on the pocket. The other boy was in the same uniform, though he had no tie and his shirttails were out. He had an expensive German-make camera around his neck.

"It's best if they do their interviews first."

"What do you want?" The boy without the camera looked steadily at Taylor.

"To find out about Declan. See if we can figure out what happened. And why."

"You're going to do some kind of Woodward and Bernstein thing? Solve the crime before the cops?" It was the same kid. He didn't sound convinced.

"I never know what I'm going to find until I find it." Taylor gestured to a chair next to a desk covered with more photos. The three teens didn't object, so he slid it closer and sat down without actually joining them at the table. Laura took a chair near the wall. He was glad she didn't crowd the interview. The girl was Carolyn Marie Bancroft and the boys were Reginald Morton and Dickie Bennett. Bennett fingered his camera and looked warily at Taylor's notebook.

"You all knew Declan?"

"We all know everyone." Morton straightened the knot of his tie. "Everyone's everyone."

"Tell me about him."

"This is only going to make it more real." Bancroft took in a breath and pressed the sleeve to her mouth. She stood and was crying before she reached the door. Laura nodded at Taylor and slipped out behind the girl.

"C'mon," Morton said. "We've all got to get real about this."

"It can be hard to deal with." Taylor moved his chair a little closer.

"Later to that. Much later. Bancroft's being a drama queen. There's going to be a whole lot of that going around. She's had a crush on McNally for—Christ, since freshman year. He ignored her. Like everyone who couldn't do something for him. She's going to forget that. Everyone's going to forget what an asshole Dec really was."

"He's dead," said Bennett. "Don't say that to the paper."

"What do you know? You took half the damn pictures for the yearbook and he didn't even know your name."

Bennett looked at the camera. "He knew it."

"What did Declan do to make you so angry?" Taylor asked.

"For one, got me nailed for cheating. The headmaster learned the answers were in my bag. Right where McNally put them. If my father weren't on the Board of Visitors, I'd be gone."

"You can prove he put them there?"

"He told me he was stealing the key to the trig midterm."

"Why'd he set you up?"

"I was a well-timed distraction. The headmaster was about to get him for all the cheating he was doing. I stayed clear after that. Only thing to do with McNally. If you don't believe me, ask some of the others. Find someone who'll be honest with you. Ask his best friend. Ronald Carlson and McNally played lacrosse together since freshman year. That didn't matter to McNally. He stole Ronald's girlfriend. Everyone talks about it."

"What's the girlfriend's name?"

"Marcella Roberts."

"Any idea where I can find her?"

"I don't know about Marcella. She's probably gone home to cry. Now I don't like to gossip …."

"No, please go on."

"McNally was selling drugs."

"How do you know that?"

"From Carolyn. She follows him around school like a puppy dog. One day he used the pay phone by the cafeteria. She heard him making a deal. He met a guy at the corner. Definitely not at Eli. Passed money for a package. Carolyn saw it all. She's such an idiot. She decided that made McNally even cooler."

"Do you know for sure there were drugs in the package?"

"I know what she said. She said it was drugs."

Morton sure wasn't holding back. Gang members showed more sympathy for the dead. Maybe Taylor was out of touch. On the police beat, he didn't spend time interviewing upper class kids. Anyone upper class really.

"Any idea what happened to Declan after he left his house Sunday night?"

"I don't even know *how* he died. We're hearing some pretty freaky stuff."

"You didn't see him that night?"

"No way, man. I was home. I went out Monday night."

"Were you with anyone?"

"Sure. Eight of us went to see *The Towering Inferno*. It was the monthly meeting of the Eli Drive-In Movie Club." He squeezed his hands together. "We're kids, so we don't understand death. Right? We're supposed to go all to pieces. Run to our parents and cry all day and night. My grandparents died. The things that were said. All the bad stuff was left out. Gone. That's what we're supposed to do with death."

"You're just being honest then?"

"Because of all this bullshit hypocrisy."

Taylor turned to Bennett. "What do you know about Declan?"

"I won't lie. I've heard some things. I've seen some things too. Why do we have to talk about that now? He's got family—"

"Climbers, all of them." Morton walked to the door. "He didn't belong at this school. New money. A family of political hacks and flatfoots. Real goddamn grunters. When my father heard Declan was coming here, he about dumped the Scotch on the rocks in his lap. He says there's a reason Eli is selective."

He left.

Bennett went to the table piled with black-and-white prints. He brushed his hand over the photos, moving sheets from side to side, uncovering different pictures, shifting, looking at others. He pulled out one, then two more. He handed them over and narrated as Taylor flipped through the headshots. "Marcella Roberts. Ronald Carlson. Martin van der Meer."

Taylor looked up at the third name.

"He's the lacrosse captain. He'll know as much as Ronald. He's the one guy on the team better than Declan. Martin winning to be captain was the only time Declan got beat at anything. To be honest, I don't think you'll find out what happened here at the school. It's out there." Bennett looked through the leaded glass window at Central Park covered in snow. "I understand you have to ask. It would make a much better story if kids were involved."

The boy shook his head and left. He was right; it would. Why did Bennett take the trouble to pick out the headshots yet say almost nothing? Did his silence mean more than Morton's anger? Was he pointing to something? Right now, Taylor needed to get to more students before the building emptied for the day. Other reporters wouldn't be far behind, and then the TV stations. They'd put McNally's schoolmates through the Eyewitness News mill, trampling over everyone and everything.

Outside the office, natural light brightened the hallway from windows on the left. Taylor passed small knots of students talking quietly. They glanced over as he passed; here was another stranger among them after news of a death. He tried to talk to a pair of boys, but they backed away as soon as he identified himself. He didn't push it. As soon as school officials found out he was here, he'd lose his shot at finding out anything else.

Laura came up from behind. "The gym?"

"Yes. What did Carolyn say?"

"He should have been lacrosse captain. He was the very best. At everything, apparently."

"She didn't wish him dead, then?"

"Not at all. He was the bad boy, and she liked him for it."

"Any details?"

"Drug dealing. She said he went up to Columbia and sold to Eli alumni. At least, that was the word from the younger brothers and sisters of alumni. Guess he was smart enough not to do it here. Carolyn saw him trade a wad of cash for a package over on Madison."

"That backs up what Reginald Morton told me, whatever his motives. Great reporting."

Her face reddened at the praise, and the flush moved down her neck to the top of her chest. His eyes lingered there a moment before he looked down the hall. They set off in the direction of practice.

The highly polished gym floor reflected boys moving in patterns and swinging sticks that spat out balls. They zigzagged, stopped, turned, caught, and hurled. The sport was alien to Taylor. Growing up, he played stickball and handball and the other games invented for concrete and tight spaces. These boys wore pads and helmets like those for football. They wielded the sticks like weapons. Looked like a great way for well-off kids to beat on each other.

The bleachers were maple-colored and shiny like the floor. Twenty or so kids watched the practice. The basketball hoops gave the gym a modern touch, with the clear Plexiglas backboards the ABA used. Up high in the far wall, the winter sun split into reds, blues, golds, purples and greens as it came through a stained glass window. Figures running, rowing and wrestling surrounded the school crest. This gym was a temple.

A coach in a white sports shirt and tight blue shorts yelled instructions. Except for "hustle" and "faster," Taylor didn't understand a thing. The whistle blew, and the running stopped. Boys pulled their helmets off. Their hands fell to their knees as they blew hard. Taylor picked out Ronald Carlson and Martin van der Meer.

"I'm going to interview those two. See if you can get anything out of these kids watching." He walked over. "Can I talk with you about Declan McNally?"

The teens became somber.

"You are …?" asked van der Meer.

"Taylor with the *Messenger-Telegram*."

"What do you want to know?"

"I understand he was a good lacrosse player."

"He was one of our best. It's a blow to the team. To the whole school." Van der Meer stood half a head taller than Carlson and just even with Taylor. His muscled torso stretched a gray practice T-shirt tight across his chest.

"He wanted to be captain, but you beat him out, right?"

"That was the coach's decision. An honor. I already told you. Declan was one of our best players."

"Were you friends?"

"We were teammates. Nothing's more important than that. What's the point of this?"

"His death is suspicious. I'm trying to figure out what happened to him." Taylor pointed at Carlson with his pen. "He was your best friend?"

"Yeah, for a long time." Carlson's close-set blue eyes made him look angry. There was a nasty purple-brown bruise under his left eye.

"How did you feel when he started dating Marcella Roberts?"

"You think I did something to Declan because of Marcella?" Carlson edged closer.

Van der Meer swung his stick onto his shoulder, at the ready.

"I was done with Marcella. She was welcome to go with anyone she wanted. You have no right coming in here and asking questions like this."

Something whistled past Taylor's head, lifting his hair. The lacrosse ball smacked the gym wall and bounced right back at him. In the same instant, van der Meer's stick swung toward Taylor's face. He ducked, but van der Meer wasn't aiming for him. Instead, the big teenager caught the ball. Everyone nearby laughed as Taylor came up from a crouch.

"What are you doing talking to *my* players?" The coach tossed and caught a second ball. He strode up to Taylor and the two boys. "Nobody talks to my players without my permission. Heads up, Carlson!" The coach whipped the second ball in Taylor's direction, and this time, before he could even think of ducking, the mesh net at the end of Carlson's stick caught the ball at chest height. "Little slow, Carlson. Or maybe not slow enough. Now both of you get showered."

They walked off, laughing.

"Leave my gym now. Or I can find a police officer."

Laura joined him at the gym doors.

"The kids tell you anything?"

"Couple might have. You were putting on too good a show. Apparently no one interrupts coach's practice. Ever."

"He's being protective, that's all. The two boys, though. There is something there. I need to talk with them again. You never know when a relationship is involved."

"C'mon, Taylor. These kids go for melodrama, not tragedy."

He found the words his father shoved into his head years earlier. " 'All thoughts, all passions, all delights. Whatever stirs this mortal frame. All are but ministers of Love. And feed his sacred flame.' "

"Quoting poetry now? There are depths to you I don't know."

"Coleridge, from 'Love.' We all act on passions. Even these kids. Maybe Carlson killed McNally over the girl."

"If you say so. Sounds like a stretch to me. When did you learn *those* lines?"

"I'll tell you all about that someday. My father recited Coleridge a lot. Over drinks. Lots and lots of drinks."

"My quote for you, from Tolstoy. 'Happy families are all alike; every unhappy family is unhappy in its own way.' "

"You come to school, you learn so much."

"Keep studying. You'll get there."

Why did he bring up the damn poem? He didn't need those lines to make the point. To show Laura how smart he was while standing in a school that was so much more her element? If so, he was actually an idiot.

Taylor pushed open the door to the icy golden air of the late afternoon and held it for Laura.

"Let's eat down in the Village," she said as she walked out ahead of him. "We're still getting drinks, right?"

"I may be out sick, but I think I can manage."

"You look all right to me. CBGB has The Ramones and Patti Smith. It'll be a blast."

He turned east toward Lex. "CB what?"

"Don't play like you don't know. It's *the* punk rock club."

"I guess these aren't the same punks from my old neighborhood in Queens."

"Funny you should mention it. The Ramones are from Forest

Hills. They're the best. Fast, angry, funny rock and roll. It's *the* answer to disco and all that old hippie stuff."

"Careful. That old hippie stuff is *my* refuge from disco."

11

———— ◆ ————

TAYLOR PULLED OPEN the door to Ray's Pizza on Broadway at Bleecker. "Lou Reed and Velvet Underground. They rock and roll."

They'd talked music the entire ride down on the subway.

"See, you like punk after all. The Underground invented it. Oh, everyone argues. I know. They came first."

"*Rock 'n' Roll Animal* is the all time number one live album. All time."

"Exactly."

Taylor had Laura get a booth while he ordered two slices for himself and one for her, a Tab, and a Miller High Life. He folded one slice in half and polished it off quickly. It tasted so good. Laura looked on, bemused, and worked on hers more slowly.

"Now, what do we have?" He sat back, opened the notebook and drank the beer.

"Well, I think the two Eli boys—"

"No, we need to think about this from the beginning. Figure out what we're missing." He flipped the narrow pages. "Declan McNally leaves his house Sunday night after arguing with his father. His mom says they fight a lot."

"So do all teenagers."

"He's found dead early Tuesday morning in the Meatpacking District wearing Mark Voichek's field jacket. He's frozen from the inside out. In fact, his underwear is frozen to him."

"Someone wanted him to look homeless."

"That's one theory. Whoever did it was hoping the system would swallow him up. That he'd be buried without anyone taking notice. It's not a crazy plan, given we're talking about Bellevue. Still, we won't know for sure until we have a cause of death. You can bet Quirk is working hard on that tonight."

"It's possible he put the clothes on himself and died sometime after."

"Right. So it *could* be exposure. Changes the whole story."

"Or maybe someone thought they were killing a homeless boy."

"How or why did he get wet?"

"I think that happened when he was inside somewhere. It's too cold outside to get wet. So he put those clothes on—"

"Or someone dressed him."

"After he was dead?"

"Maybe he was murdered, soaked down in his skivvies and dumped outside in the clothing. Fits with trying to hide the murder." Taylor tapped his Bic against the notebook. He loved this. Pizza, beer, and the facts of the crime. Nothing better. "The key right now is Voichek. It's his jacket. Maybe they're his jeans and sweater too. He must have seen Declan McNally sometime between Sunday night and his death. Maybe he was the last person to see him. Maybe he's the killer."

"Why put his clothes on the kid? The jacket would ID him as the murderer."

"Yeah, and he loved that thing. That's what Jansen said. It's always about connections. These two are connected. Voichek's on the run from something. That's connected too. I know it."

"What *was* the cause of death, if not exposure?"

"Wish we knew." He picked up the second slice. "Can you go to Bellevue tomorrow and see what they found?"

"Sure."

"Try to get to Quirk. He was quick to decide Declan was a homeless person when the body came in. He's got every reason to try and look good now."

Taylor finished the beer. He shouldn't like these full-sized bottles. They broke the rule. But the first one tasted good, and he wanted another. Figuring out the McNally story was his idea of a good time. Laura's too, judging from the way her warm dark eyes regarded him. He got up absently and remembered to come back and ask Laura if she wanted anything.

"A Michelob this time. You've got that 'looking down into the crime scene' stare."

"I'm sorry, it's—"

"No, I like it. The intensity."

He returned with both beers and leaned all the way back against the chair. He'd read enough of the notes. "The Gansevoort. Why there? Harry Jansen swears it's a no-go zone for the homeless. The mafia boys roust anyone who tries to hang out."

"We need to be sure it's murder. I'll get to Quirk tomorrow. Long as I get my research done, Worthless doesn't care what side projects I work. They're not trying to fire me."

The reminder he was running out of time came almost as a shock. He'd gotten so comfortable planning their next steps. What could he do? Panic? There was no point. There was no going back. The only option was to think of nothing else but getting a story no one in that newsroom could ignore. The death of Declan McNally could be that.

"Okay, the kids from school. Reginald Morton says McNally was a cheat and a drug dealer. That's some nice list of activities for a high school kid. All at a place like Eli. Were there drugs at Dalton?"

"Sure. Private school kids get the best stuff. Didn't you know?"

"I did not."

"I stuck with weed, but oh, what good weed."

Taylor laughed. "Hippie."

"Sometimes I wished I'd stayed one." Her voice was tinged with regret. Taylor wanted to ask if there was a path not taken by Laura Wheeler, but she got a question out first. "In Queens?"

"Beer, always beer."

"Still the case, I note."

"I'm trying to shrink my consciousness, not expand it. I already see enough of what's going on in the world." That was way too serious. Why was it that the instant she brought up Queens, he got insecure? Private schooling, college degree, Eastside money. All good reasons to think she was out of his league. *Drop it. Talk about the story.* "See if you have better luck getting Dickie Bennett, that yearbook photographer, to say something."

"I know. Get any details there are on the drugs. Get anything else that might point to a killer. You got it, Chief."

"I'm not your chief."

"No, you're not. What am I?"

"About my only friend at the paper right now."

"You've got Mrs. Wiggins."

"Yeah, exactly." *Now, what to say?* "You're my partner on this story for as long as I've got a job."

"That's not much of a deal, the way you're going."

"Says a lot about your judgment."

He bought another round and they talked more about the story, the cop shop and other newsroom gossip, whiling away a relaxed hour until Laura said they could get into CBGB and continue drinking there while they waited for the Ramones to come on.

Outside, a light snow drifted through the air, which was cold yet mercifully still. They walked east to get to the Bowery, paused to wait for a gap in the traffic and trotted across Lafayette. A Checker cab honked, and Taylor threw the driver a friendly finger.

The East Village closed in on them as they went. Dark and impoverished. It was a very different city here, a foreign one. The skyscrapers and 24-hour lights of midtown were gone from sight. It was easy to disappear down one of these narrow streets and show up the next day in the police blotter. Taylor and Laura passed figures flitting by on the sidewalk. Vagrants, squatters, addicts. Possible muggers? They approached 315 Bowery from across the street. The sign read "CBGB" with "OMFUG" below it, in red capital letters the typeface of a circus poster.

"What does it mean?" he asked.

"Country Bluegrass Blues and Other Music for Uplifting Gormandizers."

"Really?"

"It's all the *other* music now. Hilly only books punk and art rock, which is punk anyway. There's a huge debate about that, of course. I mean what is the band Television, punk or art rock?"

"I'm going to sound like an old fart if I say I watch mine, right?"

"Worse."

He pulled open the door. The stench of the stalest, oldest beer from spills never cleaned up mixed with cigarette smoke, new and ancient, and sweat clobbered him. His shoes made a gummy smack coming off the floor as he moved over to a small glass window. He paid the woman ten bucks. Laura tried to argue over this, so he said she could buy drinks, never intending to let her. Inside, the bar appeared to be built out of scavenged plywood. Only a few people were drinking at this point. Blue, red, and gold neon Pabst, Miller, and Michelob signs floated above the bar, giving eerie light to the dark, narrow space. They provided Taylor some comfort in these alien surroundings. Ahab's had the same signs, after all. Through a door at the back of the bar was an opening into a room with a small stage lit a bit better than the bar. Silver microphone stands, the only objects on the black stage, glinted in the light. He wanted to stay here, safe under the beer signs.

Laura took a seat on one of the stools. She waved her hand to offer the next one, as if they were somewhere far more formal.

"I have this theory, an idea at least." He sat down. "There's something that happens without warning. I can't say exactly when. In one instant your music is the soundtrack of the moment, of the world. In the next, it's in the oldies bin."

"I said you'll like the Ramones."

He eyed three punks drinking PBRs.

"Everyone obsesses on the leather and the pierced ears and noses because those make for great photo spreads. Even in *Rolling Stone*, which is so old fart now. It's not about all that. It's about stripping everything away and getting to the music. The Ramones could be the Beach Boys if those guys had been really, really angry. And from Queens. Wait till you hear 'Rockaway Beach.' "

He laughed and took a swig of his seven-ounce Rolling Rock. His three-beer buzz had vanished as soon as they left Ray's and walked through the cold. As he drank now, the fizzy lager woke up the buzz and put him at lightheaded ease. With a few more, he might even get comfortable here. Hell, he could get comfortable anywhere. Wasn't that the point? "I've been thinking about the boy's family."

"Do you ever let go of a story, and you know, relax?"

"I'm not sure I do." He didn't.

Laura sipped vodka and cranberry through a thin straw. She'd broken one of Taylor's drinking rules. Never, ever mix.

He didn't tell her that, since the rules only applied to him. Besides, one of the rules was he didn't tell people he needed rules. "The father, Constable, handles the legal end of the city's purchasing. That's hundreds of millions of dollars worth of business. Often dirty business. The grandfather, Big Johnny, he's another one. He's got more enemies than Nixon had on his little list. What if Declan's murder was an attack on the family?"

"That's a new theory."

"Gotta have theories." He waved to the bartender for another Rolling Rock.

The crowd grew as they talked. Kids in their late teens and early twenties pressed up against the bar. The noise in the place seemed to leap to a roar all at once. Leather everywhere—jackets, pants, vests, halters—and various horror-show hairstyles, short and spiky, plus a couple of bristling Mohawks. It was funny all the same. The Mohawks aside, the leather and slicked hair reminded Taylor of the greasers who stalked his neighborhood a decade and a half ago. Of course, none of those kids stuck safety pins through their noses. And none of these kids looked like they were up to sticking you with a knife. They weren't poor or working class. All the stuff they wore cost money.

"We should go in the back before it gets too crowded," Laura said.

He bought two more beers and another Cape Codder for her and followed her lead as she squeezed through the crowd, which was tight-packed but friendly. He parked himself beside Laura at the back wall. They were at most twenty feet from the tiny stage. Punks in leather with sculpted hair and shiny baldheads crowded the dance floor. The Ramones stalked onto the stage, beat-up leather jackets and clouds of black hair, and slashed their way through three songs in less than five minutes. The tunes were brutally loud and lightning fast. The kids on the floor jumped up and down in a primal tribal bop. He glanced at Laura, worried she'd want to join that mass, but she watched, fascinated. Underneath the noise, he made out the words to a song the greasers actually would have sung if they'd known it. "Rock 'n' Roll High School." It was almost like the boys from his neighborhood returned from the musical dead, furious at what the seventies had done to their sound. The storm of music crashed over him. It wasn't alien or foreign, just good old rock and roll. He liked it.

They finished in 20 minutes, the fastest set of the fastest songs. They gave way to Patti Smith, who was fiercely, proudly ugly. Rail thin with long black hair, she could have easily been another Ramone. She played a bit slower, but as loud and with as much fury. Smith launched into a cover of "Gloria," the classic written by Van Morrison while he was a member of Them.

"I love this song."

"What?" She put a hand on his shoulder.

He leaned down. "I love this song."

"Oh, so do I! See? You *are* a punk."

"Guess I am."

His mouth met hers. They kissed tentatively and would have kept at it, but a trio of bounding punks pushed them apart. They were barely able to stay next to each other as the bouncing crowd jumped and thumped through the end of the concert.

Taylor climbed—fell almost—into the backseat of the cab after Laura. Once the cab pulled away, she leaned against his shoulder, looking across him out the window. Cars, streetlights, traffic signals, and signs passed, fuzzy blurs of light. He kissed her, and she pressed against him and sighed. He put his arm around her shoulders. They contorted into the awkward sideways necking required by the confines of a New York taxi. Spine-twisting it might have been, but it was good and long and ended as they pulled up to a row of walkups on Third Avenue just above 77th.

She unlocked the red steel front door of the four-story building. Taylor stepped over Chinese delivery menus and four-color fliers carpeting the entryway and followed as Laura started up the stairs, her rear end swaying as they climbed. She unlocked her apartment door on the fourth floor. They walked down the hall past the kitchen and entered the living room, where they both dropped onto a futon couch that looked like a big folded noodle.

"Man, you hike that every day."

She laughed and picked up a big jug of red wine by the glass loop. "Wine?"

"You wouldn't have anything in the way of a beer?"

"You think this is Queens?'

"No, definitely not Queens." He shook his head a bit too hard. His brain sloshed around in his skull. This was about the time of night he started breaking his rules. "Sure, why not."

"I'll get glasses." She tried to rise from the noodle and fell back.

He caught her by the hips.

"Whoa. Bit unsteady there." Once up, she went down the hall to the kitchen.

The compact living room was comfortable and neat. A small TV with rabbit ears sat on a table in the corner. Two impressionist prints were tacked to the wall. A component stereo system included amp, tape deck, and turntable. Taylor flipped record albums in a blue milk crate. New York Dolls, Ramones, Television. Farther back, he tipped past The Beatles, The Doors, Velvet Underground, John Denver. John Denver?

"Goddammit Sarah Jane, you have got to wash the dishes." The sound of running water.

At the back of the carton, he found *Simon and Garfunkel's Greatest Hits*, the album everyone ended up with, one way or the other. Taylor had two, an LP and a cassette. Both gifts from women. They'd left. Simon and Garfunkel had stayed.

Laura came in and poured wine in a tall glass and handed it over. On it, Fred Flintstone chased Barney Rubble.

"Nice wine glass."

"They were grape jelly jars. Sarah Jane says they remind her of home."

"She's from Bedrock?"

"Almost. St. Louis."

She sat on the couch. He held up the John Denver. "This hers too?"

"No, that's mine."

"John Denver isn't very punk." He sipped the wine. Mixing was a one-way ticket to next-day disaster, but it tasted good and was going down warm and relaxing like red wine always did. It was a different sort of buzz from beer. Maybe he needed to have it more often. Anyway, he couldn't let Laura drink alone.

"You don't know? He's a very, very angry man."

"At the songs he's forced to sing?"

"Makes sense, doesn't it?" She drank from her Flintstones glass. "I bought it in high school. My musical tastes have changed a whole lot since."

"Because that was *so* long ago." He kissed her and kept his arm around her after. She leaned against him. "Why did you keep the album? I mean, if your tastes changed so much?"

"There are times I like it, when I'm alone, when no one's judging whether my music fits their urban nihilistic vision."

"Sometimes too much of nothing?"

"Yeah, guess so. What I want right now is for you to stay the night."

"I'd like that."

She led the way to the bedroom with its twin beds, one against each wall. One was made up, one covered in clothes. She took his glass, set it down on a small dresser with hers, came close and undid his belt. He kissed her and pulled her blouse from her skirt.

The apartment door banged opened. Two laughing voices entered. Stumbling.

"C'mon. Get your ass up," said a woman's voice.

Laura frowned, moved to close the bedroom door, but as she got there, a blond woman pushed inside. She had the pretty face of a farm-fed Midwesterner and wore jeans slashed up and down the legs.

"I have the room tonight," said the woman.

"You know I've never asked for it before."

"I put in for tonight and no one objected. They're *your* rules, Laura."

"I know. Just tonight can—"

"No, I can't. C'mon in."

The man entered the crowded room, smiled and stretched out on the bed covered in laundry. "They can stay. I don't mind a crowd." He was rail-thin, with a shaved head, except for the frill of a Mohawk.

"Why can't you go to his house?"

"His parents kicked him out." The blonde dropped her coat to the floor.

"Parents can be tough on the anarchist lifestyle," said Taylor.

"Silly old man." The boyfriend pulled Sarah Jane down on top of him and groped for her rear as he applied his lips to hers with some diligence.

"Let's go." Laura grabbed Taylor's hand and pulled him out of the room. "We can hang out for a while, at least until Annie gets home."

They went back to the living room.

"Where does she sleep?"

"On the futon. Sarah Jane and I share the bedroom, except when someone needs it for privacy. I thought she'd give me a break tonight."

"Who was that *old* guy?" the boyfriend loudly asked Sarah Jane.

"I don't know. Someone from the paper. Probably her boss."

A low moaning started, followed by a rocking banging to the unmistakable rhythm.

This killed Taylor's desire. The red wine buzz began the quick slide into a hangover. If Annie came home, he'd be really uncomfortable. "I should go."

"With roommates it's difficult, you know …. Can we go to your place?"

The Airstream in the driveway of his burnt-out house? No, not on the first date. There were more embarrassing things than roommates.

"Not tonight."

She looked hurt.

"You know. I'm still trying to get the place fixed up."

"I didn't mean this to be a turnoff."

"It wasn't a turnoff at all. It's late. I've got work to do tomorrow. I need to break something on the story before Worth figures out a way to finish firing me."

He kissed her a last time and moved to the door as the racket in the bedroom reached its crescendo. The look on her face was sad, but not angry. Loneliness descended as he walked down the stairs. A night with Laura had been right there before him, about to happen. The goddamn trailer would be cold even with its jury-rigged heater. Cold and empty of company and lacking the welcome light of a real room. He didn't even feel like drinking more to push away this sadness. He'd passed the point of no return. He caught a cab and handed over half a day's pay for the ride to Forest Hills. The lights out the window were harsh and hurt his eyes—nothing like the blurred entertainment of the ride up from CBGB.

PART IV:
Friday, March 14,
1975

12

———◆———

T HE ELEVATOR OPENED directly onto a vestibule. Marcella Roberts lived with her parents and sister at East 87ᵗʰ, in an apartment on the 14ᵗʰ floor. The Roberts' flat was, in fact, the entire floor, a four-bedroom home on one level. Taylor had called ahead. The father was at work, the mother at a meeting to plan Eli Prep's memorial service for Declan McNally. This could work to Taylor's advantage.

The housekeeper entered the room as soon as the elevator door closed. "You're doing a story about that poor boy?"

"Yes."

"It's so sad. Terrible." She sounded liked she meant it. She went to get Marcella.

While he waited, Taylor walked off the vestibule to check its size. One and a half Airstreams.

The rug, the table along the wall and the gilt-framed paintings of flowers, horses, and huntsmen all looked old and expensive. He moved closer to a still life to see the brush strokes in the oil paint.

"You like it? It bores me. Like all this gilded crap." Marcella Roberts' face was striking, with hazel eyes and thin, dark lips.

She wore a black leather jacket over a black T-shirt lettered with something he couldn't read and tight jeans that narrowed down her slender legs.

"Thank you for seeing me."

"We'll see." A world-weary sigh from a girl too young for one. "I'm not sure I want to say much."

She led him through three rooms to a small study with a desk and bookshelves. She sat with legs crossed on the desk chair. He took the only other seat, a small uncomfortable wooden chair designed to encourage guests to make visits brief. The single floor-to-ceiling window was framed by ruby drapes with shears drawn.

"What are you going to write?" Marcella asked.

"It depends on what I find."

"You're trying to figure out who did it, right? The fucking pigs never will. Declan said all kinds of people get away with murder. Declan said the smart cops are all taking bribes because they need to. Just to survive the system. Which is completely falling apart anyway."

"That's surprising to hear. Declan's father and grandfather were cops. His brother still is."

"He wasn't talking about his family. Well, I don't think he was."

"What did Declan say about his father?" Taylor wanted more about the argument at the McNally's Sunday night. He didn't know enough about what went on inside that house.

"According to *him*, Declan could never do anything right. Mr. McNally has this big thing about how he came up from nowhere. He got his law degree while still a cop. He moved them from Queens to the Upper Eastside. Declan was somehow supposed to do the same thing, even though it was his father who put him in Eli. There's no bootstrapping in our school. We're already up. It was like Mr. McNally was angry at the opportunities he created for Declan. I don't know how to explain it exactly. It doesn't make sense. Whatever choices

Declan made, they were the wrong ones."

A tear spilled down her cheek, then another. She put her face in her folded arms. Her narrow shoulders gently heaved.

The laughter of Taylor's own father returned. "A copyboy? I expected something ridiculous, but you've always found ways of exceeding my low expectations for you. Congratulations, copy-BOY." The professor mixed himself another vodka tonic and began reciting Samuel Taylor Coleridge's poem, "Christabel."

If that's what Declan had to deal with, Taylor could understand the boy's anger. "Mr. McNally said he and Declan argued over homework on Sunday night. That Declan blew up and ran out of the house."

"Declan was upset afterward. That man rode and rode Declan about everything."

"You saw Declan Sunday night?"

"He came here. He stayed the night in the guest room."

"When did he leave?"

"I've told the police all this. He ate breakfast. Said he'd see me at school. That was the last time we talked. He didn't come to Eli on Monday."

"Your parents knew he was here?"

"Of course. They liked him very much. They didn't care for his father."

"Did the arguments between Declan and his father ever get violent?"

"He never hit him. Not that I know of. He was just such a goddamn hypocrite. Fuck, I'm so sick of all the hypocrisy." She took a Kleenex from a silver box and wiped her nose. "I need a break from the girls who don't get it. Their mothers too. 'Oh dear, how sad you must be.' Then they start wailing and telling me how fucking terrible *they* feel." Her pain was real and easier to see the harder she tried to stay in control. She squeezed her knees. "You'll find out who did it to him? Get to the truth?

That's most important. Declan always said what's true is all that matters."

He'd dig out all the facts he could. He never promised anyone the truth. He wasn't going to start with this sad teenage girl.

"What do you believe happened?"

"He was murdered."

"Why do you think that?"

"It must be. I mean everything we're hearing. They found him dumped on the street. Dressed like a homeless person. Someone did *that* to him."

"Something happened to Declan. That's certain. How long had you two been dating?"

"Dating? You think we go to sock hops?"

"Eli? More like cotillions."

"We were *with* each other. It was simple."

"For how long?"

"About four weeks."

"You were *with* Ronald Carlson before that?"

"Yes."

"When did it end with Ronald?"

"Five weeks ago." She fiddled with the corner of the silver tissue box, seemed to catch her own reflection in it. Puffy eyes. Black streaks from running mascara. She shook her head and turned away.

"So a week between the two?"

"I got bored with Ronald. I became very interested in Declan."

"How did Ronald take it?"

"You should definitely talk to him. And that bully van der Meer."

"Why?"

"They attacked Declan last week. Beat him up badly. We were supposed to meet after lacrosse, and he showed up an hour late with a bloody nose and a bruised face. He claimed it was just a tough practice."

"How do you know it wasn't?"

"I heard from others. The three of them had a screaming argument. Coach broke it up. Declan was fine when he left the gym. Ronald and Martin followed him."

"If Ronald thought Declan convinced you to leave—"

"I make my own choices."

"Do you think Ronald attacked Declan because of you?"

" 'Because' doesn't matter. He did it. Him and van der Meer. I told you that."

"Did they kill him?"

At this question, her adult pose collapsed. She picked up a homemade rag doll on the shelf and held it. "I don't know. Maybe. They're stupid boys. I didn't think Ronald was that angry." She started crying again. "I'm sorry. I'm so tired of being sad. I know it's only starting."

"Any idea where I can find Carlson and van der Meer after school today?"

She looked at a clock on the shelf. "It's TGIF. Once practice is done, try the Blarney Rock at 44th and Eighth Avenue. Say around five. That's their happy hour."

"Not the place I'd expect."

"They think they're slumming. And they don't get proofed."

13

---◆---

THE SKY WAS the inky blue of dusk turning into evening when Taylor reached the corner of 44th and Eighth. The temp was supposed to be higher than yesterday, but the AP weatherman got that wrong. He used a phone booth to try Laura at the paper; she was still out. Maybe she was working the leads they'd discussed. What if he'd screwed things up last night when he didn't take her back to his trailer? That was just like him. Mess up a relationship before it even got started. He made another call to Harry Jansen's pay phone number. No news on Mark Voichek. More frustration. His best lead was going cold. He considered putting a story about Voichek in the paper to see what flushed out. A tip maybe. Or Voichek himself. Laura could byline the piece. No, he didn't want to give away the one advantage he had over everyone else. Not yet. Anyway, how would Worth react if Laura filed a story? He'd probably go after her for working with Taylor. He wouldn't let that happen.

The blue neon "B" flickered in the sign over the Blarney Rock. He entered, and murky darkness dropped over him like a blanket. Cigars and steam-tray food filled the air. He stood for a minute to let his eyes adjust. As they did, small pools of yellow light illuminated at his feet from low-watt bulbs recessed into the black ceiling. They led to the bar.

The two schoolboys were there, both in khakis and button-downs, their school jackets slung over bar stools. They giggled as they waved around drinks of a washed-out cola color. Probably rum. Carlson and van der Meer both held cigarettes in that obvious way kids did when they wanted others to notice they were smoking.

One stool away sat an old man in a battered blue suit. His head moved like it was on a swivel given too much lubrication. He snatched at a shot glass full of something clear, parked its edge carefully at his anemic lower lip, and slowly tipped the contents into his mouth. He set the glass down. Liquor ran down his chin. He didn't bother to wipe.

"Know what you're tryin' to do," the old man slurred and lurched against the bar. "You're trying to get me snockered. Thass not polite company."

The boys laughed louder. Van der Meer's was a strange wheeze for a boy in such a big body, and Carlson's was a cruel snicker.

"Get our friend another." Carlson waved at the bartender. "Whatever's next down."

"Cancel that." Taylor stepped to the bar. "They're underage. Cokes, and I mean *just* Cokes for them."

The sleepy-looking bartender hesitated a moment, put two RC Colas in front of the boys, and picked up their half-finished drinks.

"What are you ruining our fun for?" asked Carlson.

"Fun, is it?"

"Yeah." The cruel laugh again. "The old man said he could drink *anything*. So we took him up on it. We're going down the bar one bottle at a time. That was gin. Was that gin?"

"Yeah, gin," said van der Meer.

"This a regular after-school activity for you two? Mixing with the masses and killing them with your kindness?"

"Get away from us, man." Van der Meer waved at the door. "We don't have to talk to you. Not at all. Coach said so."

Cruelty, youth, and money were such an ugly combination. He didn't like these boys. That wasn't enough to put them in the story. *Let go of the anger. Go for the facts.*

"I can talk to your parents instead. Ask them about your regular Friday evening party here at the Blarney Rock."

Carlson took a sip of soda. Van der Meer frowned and did the same. Was the bigger boy always the follower? He had more of the bluster. Carlson might be quiet, but maybe he was the one in charge.

"Why are you bothering us?" van der Meer asked.

"I want to know what happened between you two and Declan."

"Told you at school. Nothing."

"I know there was a fight. Declan came out on the short end of that stick."

"Don't know what you're talking about."

"Use your brains, kid. When there's a girl in the middle, and people keep saying a lot of nothing, the wrong folks get the wrong idea. Cops and prosecutors. Reporters even. They all get interested. Tell me what happened."

Carlson bit his lower lip. "It's not what you think."

"Tell me and I'll let you know."

"We both were friends with Marcella. He never said a thing when we started going out. You know, that he wanted her. Then one week she's with me, the next with him. I tried to talk to her. She gives me this whole women's lib trip. Like nobody owns her."

"What did Declan say?"

"He wouldn't talk about it. Not one word. He had this way of ignoring people. He switched you off. 'I don't need to hear from you anymore.' " Carlson turned an invisible switch and gave a dismissive wave. "That's how he did it."

"So you jumped him after practice?"

"No! We went to get answers. Find out what was really going on. For the good of the team."

Van der Meer stepped away from the bar toward Taylor. "Yeah, definitely that. The prick wouldn't talk to either of us. He was a cop's boy. A nobody. Our families opened Eli."

The drunken old man slid off his stool to the floor with a muffled thump and didn't move. The two boys looked at his prone figure and started laughing again.

Taylor waved over the bartender. "Give me a hand." They lifted the dead weight and started carrying him but were immediately in a tug-of-war. The bartender pulled toward the front door and Taylor toward a booth. "What are you doing?"

"Taking him outside."

"You let these kids load him up and now you want to dump him on Eighth Avenue?"

"He'd have drunk his way there on his own."

"The kids did it. You let them. He sleeps it off in a Blarney booth."

"I got a fucking job to do here, buddy. You fall down in the bar, you're out the door. Nothing's going to change that."

"You know what? Maybe you're my story tomorrow. Feeding booze to two under-aged sons of *very* rich families. Letting them poison this guy. Was that your job today?"

"Oh, c'mon, man. You'd have to go a long way to poison Charlie. This was like a lottery win for him."

"I like that quote." Taylor gently lowered the old man's legs, leaving the bartender holding Charlie by the armpits. He took out his notebook.

"This … was … like … a … lottery … win … for … him."

"Shit."

No one had ever called Taylor on his bluff. No matter who the person was, no matter how small-time the thing they'd done. They were always sure they were the big story.

They carried Charlie to a booth, and Taylor returned to the bar. "Tell me what really happened after practice."

"He took the first swing," said Carlson.

"It was the last he took too." Van der Meer started hiccupping.

"Shut your face, Martin. Like, don't you get it? This is serious." He turned back to Taylor. "We tried to talk to him. Tried explaining how things worked."

Taylor looked up from his notebook. "The respect that a *nobody* should show his betters?"

"Nice way of putting it." Van der Meer hiccupped again.

"He wouldn't say a thing," said Carlson. "I started yelling at him. Out of nowhere he swings his lacrosse stick at my head."

"You hit him back?"

They stayed quiet.

"So he swung first and you beat him up?"

"He tried to keep swinging," said van der Meer. "We were just too fast."

"And there were two of you. Where were you on Monday?"

"In school," said Carlson. "There's a building full of teachers and students to tell you that."

"After that?"

"I was studying at Martin's house."

"Yeah, he was with me."

"Your parents?"

"Sure, they were there," said van der Meer.

"*No*," said Carlson. "They were out until eleven."

"Oh right."

"So from the end of practice until eleven you're his alibi? And he's yours?"

They both nodded.

"Convenient."

"This is crazy." Carlson picked up his jacket. "We didn't do anything to Declan. Not after the fight."

"These boys have had their last evening here," Taylor told the bartender, who was sulking in the corner. "I'm sure their fathers have very nice liquor cabinets they can pilfer."

14

———◆———

M RS. WIGGINS WORKED at a file cabinet on the right side of the morgue. Taylor took the seat at the carrel.

"Are you turning my morgue into your office?"

"I'm sorry. I need to work somewhere. Till I'm fired, at least."

"Mind how you go." She pulled her glasses off. "They don't really care what I'm up to down here. I like it that way. Did you hear? Susan Hayward died."

"That's Marmelli's problem now. There's nothing he likes better than picking through wire copy on dead celebs."

A sly smile. "Just thought you'd want to keep up."

"I'm dealing with the dead one at a time from now on. Whatever happens."

Taylor called Harry Jansen's pay phone again and finally got a break, if a small one. Jansen believed Voichek would show at Joshua Harper's memorial service the next day. Taylor would definitely attend. Laura walked into the room as he was hanging up. His face warmed.

"Hey, how are you?" His voice was too loud.

"I'm fine. You?"

"Fine. I'm fine."

"That's good."

"Good. We're both fine."

Stupid. Stupid. Why do I sound so stupid? At least Laura came down to see me. Now, how to make sure I don't blow the whole thing?

"Were you able to get to Bellevue?"

"Yes. Quirk is pissed off at you."

He chuckled. "Why?"

"He's in a load of shit, of course. For not trying hard enough to ID the kid."

"Just what that chucklehead deserves. I didn't bring that down on him. His incompetence did."

"Maybe, but I agreed with him. About you, that is. He was pleased to hear it. I think he believed helping me might somehow hurt your career."

"What career?"

"I left that part out. He started in by telling me they never get female reporters in the morgue. Made that obvious by leering. I sat quite demurely, sounded appalled at all his horrifying coroner talk, and crossed and re-crossed my legs a few times."

"I didn't think women's libbers went in for that approach." He looked at her legs.

"Are you kidding?" She crossed them and smiled. "I want this story as much as you do. So, what do you do in a man's world? Use a man's weakness against him."

"What would Katherine Graham say?"

"That she's got boys out getting her stories for her. Now, do you want the headlines or not?"

"By all means."

"Declan ingested barbiturates," Laura said. "Maybe enough to kill him. Certainly more than you'd take for medicinal or recreational purposes. It put him out a good long time. For now, they're sticking with exposure as cause of death."

Taylor nodded at this news. "He was knocked out by an overdose. That means someone soaked him down and dumped him outside. He was unconscious in sub-zero weather. Someone *was* trying to hide the murder as an accidental death."

"Possible." Laura gave the either way signal with her hand. "The police are still calling it a suspicious death. They want to call it murder. They *need* to call it murder. They can't yet. They don't know Declan didn't take the pills himself."

"No way," Taylor said. "He was killed. Really great reporting."

Laura flipped further back into her notebook. "I didn't do so well with the Eli kids. They've got a cop posted at the school's front door now. I waited, saw Carolyn Bancroft leave and tried to get her to stop. She waved me off and jumped into a chauffeured Town Car. I couldn't find Reginald Morton and got nowhere with Dickie Bennett. At least *he* didn't run away from me."

"Was he still wearing that camera?"

"Sure. He said he told you everything he knows and had nothing to add. 'Not one word.' "

Taylor frowned at this. "He told me nothing."

"It was odd. He looked uncomfortable."

"I'm sure he wants to talk about something. Doesn't know how to start."

"Took my card at least."

Taylor smiled. "The autopsy info alone is gold."

"I'm worried about you."

"I'll be fine—"

"No you won't. Upstairs they're talking about you like you're already gone." She nodded her head to the ceiling as if the newsroom were right on top of them. "Marmelli asked Worthless for a replacement."

"That lazy bastard. Obits is hardly enough work for him. Look, Worth can chuck me out on my ass. He's going to have to hire me back when we nail this story."

He wanted her to have confidence. He wasn't sure he did. The phone rang, and Mrs. Wiggins answered.

"Taylor, for you."

"Worth's tracked you down." Laura stared at the phone like it might bite.

"He's not that smart." Taylor took the receiver. "Yes."

"The man himself," said Pickwick. "I see, working out of the newspaper's morgue. How very poetical. Quite so."

"How did you find me?"

"Please, I'm Pickwick. You did well with my tip. I don't have a lot of time today. It's a bit busy."

"With what?"

"That would be telling. Why do you always ask the obvious? You should be asking the right questions. I must say I even surprised myself with this one. It'll make you happy. Take down this address. Joanna Kazka, 67 Ontario Street in Albany."

"Who's that?"

"That's the mother of Peter Pan's little friend."

"Tinker Bell?"

"Quite so."

"How do I know—"

Dial tone. Goddammit.

Without explaining, Taylor sent Laura upstairs to the newsroom to get the Criss+Cross Directory for Albany. A reporter's best friend, the directory was a reverse phone book that listed phone numbers by their street addresses. He dialed 67 Ontario and got the bartender at a place called Skipper's Bar & Grill. Yes, a mother and daughter lived in an apartment above the bar. No, he didn't know if they had a phone. No, he wouldn't go upstairs and get the mother.

15

———◆———

MAN-HIGH SNOWDRIFTS SLIPPED by on either side of the
Taconic State Parkway. It was like driving into the white
heart of a glacier. Laura slept next to Taylor in the front seat of
her car. Actually, her father's car. Actually, *one* of her father's
cars. By the time he'd made every fruitless call he could on the
Albany address, the last train to Albany had left Grand Central.
Laura readily offered the car. Taylor just as readily said yes to
that and her company on the ride.

A DJ at WKIP in Poughkeepsie called the time at quarter
to eleven, the temperature 13 degrees, and played "Lonely
People" by America, No. 5 on the Billboard chart. Could be
worse. Probably would get worse. The Top 40 station was the
best he could tune in this far up the Hudson. The rest were
overnight talk and easy listening. Next came ELO's "Can't Get
It Out of My Head." Taylor couldn't get one image out of his
head. Another empty apartment. This fool's errand would end
with Susan and Tinker Bell still missing and his career still
wrecked by their story. He refused to let himself believe he was
really close. That was the best way to avoid disappointment.
Then why go up at all? He couldn't help himself. He had to

know. He had to follow every lead, even if it meant more pain.

Laura's breathing was a soft whisper and her face stunning in repose. He reached his fingers to run them down her smooth white cheek but checked himself. He wanted to caress her but didn't want to wake her from a comfortable snooze. He looked up, whispered "shit," and braked the car firmly but without panicking. Two deer, black eyes, mouths blowing frozen mist, stared over the hood of the Buick Estate Wagon. They walked past the car slowly, as if put out by his appearance on their road. How did the animals get on the parkway despite the huge snow banks? How would they get off it? Some poor bastard was going to end up with venison in his grill.

The ride ended in front of Skipper's Bar & Grill in a residential neighborhood. The place reminded Taylor of Ahab's back in Queens, right down to the wooden ship's wheel for a sign. He and Laura hustled out of the cold and sat down at the bar. The illuminated Heileman's Old Style clock read eleven fifteen. Laura yawned and stretched. His head pounded from the anxious concentration of driving the parkway at close to seventy, scanning the flashing banks of snow and ice for more suicidal deer.

A BULKY MIDDLE-AGED man sat two stools down, a bottle of Genny Cream Ale and a plate full of chicken wings in front of him. He dipped one end of a wing in a dish of salad dressing and slurped the meat off in one go, throwing the whistle-clean bones in a red plastic bowl. Taylor hated leaving New York City. His knowledge was hard won. He liked the comfortable, smart-ass feeling of being an expert on almost anything in his city. There was no telling what he'd face here in the Yukon. All the new tribes and their strange customs. Like this chicken wing thing. He ordered a beer for himself and red wine for Laura.

When the drinks were delivered, Taylor handed the

bartender two bucks. "I called earlier about the woman who lives upstairs."

"Must've been Frankie. I came on at nine."

"Do you know the woman?"

"She comes in occasionally."

"Her name Kazka?"

"Maybe. I only know her as Joanna."

"She has a daughter?"

"Yeah, cute kid. Seems sickly though. I see them coming and going. What's this about? You two aren't cops. Can tell that."

"This a cop bar?"

"More like a drunk-and-disorderlies bar. We get a lot of visits."

"We're with the newspaper."

"Really? *Times-Union* or *Knick News*?"

"*Messenger-Telegram.*"

"Is that right? A New York paper up here? What do you know? The door to the apartment is in the back of the building."

The ease with which the bartender offered the info disappointed Taylor. He'd expected to make a greater effort to find someone hiding from him. Now he was convinced this was another setup. Had to go through the motions anyway. They finished their drinks and walked out into nearly horizontal snow. By the time they reached a green wooden door with cracked and peeling paint, they were shivering. Taylor banged. Nothing. He tried to imagine Joanna Kazka lolling up there in a heroin dream. The image wouldn't come. What if he forgot her? Then she'd really disappear. He fought a rising panic and banged harder, hand open to make the most noise. Laura gave him a look of concern.

"What in hell is going on?" yelled someone in Skipper's kitchen.

An exhaust fan next to the kitchen window blew out greasy smoke from cooking French fries and burgers.

"Hold on. I'm coming." A clumping on the stairs and the

door swung in. Taylor stared for a second at the woman whose name he knew as Susan Bell. He was more surprised than elated. He'd come to believe he'd wear the story about her daughter around his neck for the rest of his life.

"What do you want at this time of night?" The woman had added enough weight to look almost healthy and was better dressed than when he'd seen her last in a tenement apartment in Harlem.

"Are you kidding?" He stepped forward into the light. "I'm Taylor from the *Messenger-Telegram*. I interviewed you and your daughter. You disappeared."

Now it was Joanna Kazka's turn to be surprised. "You can't be here." She put her hand to her mouth with a little gasp. Her face went white. She pushed the door closed, but he slid his reporter's notebook on top of the bolt and leaned his shoulder against the door.

"I need to talk to you."

"Fuck, no!"

She ran up the stairs to the open door of the second floor apartment. Again, Taylor was just fast enough, stepping into the doorway before she could slam the door. She backed into the small living room, and her thin body started to shake. His own panic fell away, and his shoulders slumped in a sort of immediate relief. Now what? Her disappearance had wrecked his career. He hadn't thought what to do when they met again.

"I'm not going to hurt you." He held his hands out in front, realized he still held the notebook and stuffed it in his coat pocket. Laura came in the door behind him.

"I'm not worried 'bout you." A gasped sob. "If they find you here, they'll take my little girl. They'll kill me. Said they would."

"I can help you. Just tell me what's going on."

"Not saying a damn thing." She continued to shake.

"Why did you leave New York?"

"Oh god, oh god." She kept repeating it, rocking back and forth on her heels, eyes flooded and nose running. "This is never, never gonna end. Never, never."

"Please stop crying. I really don't care why you did it. Money, drugs. I don't care. I need to find the people who set me up. Where's your daughter? I want to see if she's okay."

"No!" Her eyes went large with fear. She put herself in front of the only other door in the room. "Please, let my girl sleep. This has been awful on her."

"I'm sure it has, but it's been hard on me too." He stepped toward her, anger rising in spite of his effort to stay in control. "I wrote a front-page story and then you vanished. No one I work for believes you're real. It destroyed my career."

Laura's hand squeezed his arm. "You're scaring her. You don't need to do this. I'm here. I've seen her. I can tell all of them at the *MT*. They'll *have* to give you your job back."

"Don't you understand?" He shook his head like she didn't. "That's not enough. I need to know who did this to me. That's the story I want. Or they'll come after me again."

Laura pulled slowly on his arm until he backed up one step, then two, and sat down on a battered couch, the corduroy cushions worn down to smoothness. Joanna Kazka perched on the steel folding chair that was the living room's other piece of furniture, aside from a small RCA on a card table that also held two TV dinner trays. A pine scent filled the room, in stark contrast to the stench of decaying food and unwashed bodies that had assailed him when he visited her apartment in Harlem.

"Why are you so frightened?" Laura asked.

"They check in."

"Who does?"

"This goon Jackie. Once a week at least. Different days. Different times. I never know when. I think he watches us too."

"Is he from New York?"

"No, local. He's always complaining we keep him from his Off Track Betting parlor."

The bedroom door opened and the nine-year-old girl darted

to her mother, stepping between her legs and pressing back. She too looked healthier than when Taylor had last seen her. She eyed him curiously. He moved off the couch, and as Joanna clutched at her daughter, he turned over the girl's left arm. The skin appeared healed. He checked the other. Same thing. No fresh tracks.

"Let me see her legs?"

"No, please. She stopped."

"Stopped?" he barked. The girl started crying. Taylor stepped back, appalled at what he'd done. How was he ever going to clear himself if he couldn't keep it together here? Frightening a little girl wasn't going to fix anything. He sat back and rubbed his face with his hands. He was behaving like a shit. What was the point if he had to scare this child? "I'm sorry for yelling. What's her real name? Not Tinker Bell, I'm sure."

The girl quieted. Her mother answered. "Clare. Tinker Bell was that Roger's idea."

"You mean McEaty? The guy who brought me to see you?"

"Yeah, him. I never heard his real last name."

"Did you know he wasn't a cop?"

"You kidding? Course he wasn't a damn cop. I know the smell of pig. He was some wannabe. An actor like."

"How'd you get involved with him?"

"Real cops brought him to me. A street narc named Forrester busts into the apartment one day with these two suits."

"Suits?"

"Cops too, but not narcs. They threatened to put me in jail for a long time. Take Clare away. They said I'd never find her again. I was holding enough stuff so they could do that under the new drug law. All's I had to do was talk to you. Tell you my story just like it was." She shuddered. "Only give you the wrong names. I rehearsed with Roger. He treated the whole thing like it was some kind of performance. He even had a script. If you ask me, he mighta been a grifter." She squeezed her daughter. "I didn't mean to hurt you, but I couldn't lose her."

Taylor leaned back, tired and sad. Addicts were master manipulators. Joanna was no exception. She was throwing her pain at him, looking for some kind of forgiveness. She was also fighting to survive odds he'd never faced, not even with his job on the line.

"Did you hear any other names?"

"No."

"Did they say why they were doing it?"

"They said it was some kinda practical joke."

"What did they look like?"

"The first, like every narc. Long hair, not long enough, shaggy mustache. I'd never seen him before. The suits were suits. Short hair, fat faces. One black haired, one blond. I think. I was high a lot. You met McEaty. That's what I remember."

"That's not going to help much."

"I was in bad shape. They grabbed me out of there when your story came out. I didn't expect that. They brought me up to this frozen hole. Jackie comes by with twenty-five bucks when he visits. I'm not allowed to leave until he says. And he says he doesn't know when he'll say."

"How did your daughter get off heroin?" Laura nodded at the little girl, who bit the knuckle of her thumb. She looked like an animal ready to bolt at the first hint of a threat.

"She had to do the withdrawal. I put her through it. This whole thing scared me to death. I couldn't lose her. She hurt, but it was fast."

"You?"

"I'm not as strong." A rueful smile. "I'm on methadone. It's better now. I'm sorry about what happened. Jackie showed me the articles when I got here. He said I'd made a lot of people really happy doing that to you."

Taylor moved slowly across the room to the lone window. His arms and legs were heavy. He believed Joanna, and his problems weren't anywhere near solved. In tracking her down, he hadn't found out much about who set him up. Or why. He could wait here for the guy watching over her. That might take a week. Or more. And Taylor would tip his hand and bring violence on them in the bargain.

"I want you to stay here and keep quiet about this visit. I don't know who's behind what happened. You're not safe until I do and can print every detail for half a million people to read."

Laura joined him at the window. "What about the paper?"

"They're going to have to take our word for it. That is, if I tell them anything."

"You must tell Garfield and Worth."

"I don't know that I can trust them. If it gets out we know where they are, God knows what will happen."

Honesty was the wrong policy. That was instantly clear. Joanna shrieked and stood up, backing away and pulling her daughter with her. "Oh goddamn you. You're going to get us killed!" The shaking started again. "I knew I couldn't trust you. I can't trust anyone. Goddamn you."

Taylor didn't blame her, but he had to get her to calm down. "Easy. Easy. You never saw us. We never saw you. We *will* protect your secret. You'll be safe here."

"How do I know?"

"You've already gotten this far. And that's a long way, right?"

She managed a small, pained smile. "I did get us cleaned up."

Laura walked over and crouched down to say goodbye to Clare, who held tight to Joanna's hand.

"My mommy's taking care of us."

"She sure is." Laura squeezed a little arm once. "She's going to keep doing that."

Taylor hurried them to the car, partly because of the cold but also out of concern Joanna's watcher would appear out of the snowy dark. He drove on Ontario toward downtown Albany. The dashboard clock said ten to midnight. An AM station said the temperature was seven degrees. Some serious villains had pulled Joanna into a mess. He wasn't sure he could pull her out. Or himself. But knowing something was better than the void of the past eight weeks.

"They may kill her anyway. I don't think she'll ever be safe here."

"She's as safe as she can be." Laura her hand on his. "There's nothing more you can do now. Were you serious? You're really not going to let the paper know? Not even Garfield?"

"Not until I can guarantee their safety. I can't go to the cops because the guys who set me up are cops. Besides, who'd put her in protective custody because she hoaxed a reporter? They'd just laugh at me. Or throw a party."

"Then Worth's going to fire you," she looked out the window, "on Monday."

"He may. I'm sure as hell not getting Joanna and her daughter killed to save my job." He withdrew his hand to rub the bridge of his nose and put it back on top of hers. Too many unanswered questions rattled around in his head. He was exhausted from thinking. He was playing a game against several unseen, unknown opponents without any idea of the rules. "We should stay over here and get up and drive early. Tomorrow is Declan McNally's funeral and the memorial service for Joshua Harper. Voichek is the break we really need."

He pulled up to the Wellington Hotel on State Street. He'd stayed here on a previous trip to track down a Queens assemblyman who'd bribed his way out of a hit-and-run. That story pissed off the party hacks, pissed off the political reporters at the paper and pissed off the cops. All for nothing; the case vanished somewhere inside the Queens DA's office.

"I'll get us rooms."

"Get us one." She kissed him.

He got out and handed the car keys to a bellhop. The wind howled down the avenue in front of the old hotel as he came around to the sidewalk.

"Christ, I thought New York was cold."

"It'll be warmer soon." She looped her arm in his.

Taylor took a room key from the sleepy desk clerk, who roused himself long enough to leer at both of them. Wasn't leering supposed to be over with? When was he ever going to get any benefit from the sexual revolution? Far as he could tell, it hadn't happened. He unlocked the door and turned on the light. The room was decorated on the opulent side of Victorian, with lots of drapes and pillows and marble. He slid off his coat and helped Laura off with hers. She turned the light off and switched on a small reading lamp.

"Need to get the lighting right."

"Yes."

He stepped close to her. "We're going to live up to the look that clerk gave us."

"I hope so."

He kissed her and caught the scent of flower blossoms, not too heavy, coming off her wavy brown hair. They were in bed, undressed, and under the covers quickly, driven by both the cold and their desire. He did his best to slow down, but it was still first-time lovemaking, a mix of guesswork, anxiety, and passion. He'd gone a long time without. He'd thought about this since he left Laura's apartment in disappointment the night before. He wasn't disappointed now.

PART V:
Saturday, March 15, 1975

16

———◆———

TAYLOR WOKE WITH a sudden start, a rearing leap to befuddled consciousness. It happened whenever he slept in an unfamiliar place. It still happened in the trailer, at least when he didn't drink enough. His subconscious wouldn't get used to the Airstream. He didn't blame it. Laura's light, even breathing came from next to him, the same sound of living energy as when she dozed in the car on the ride up. That's right. They'd gone to Albany, to track down a junkie and her daughter. Would it be enough? Could he help the two of them? He slipped out of bed, reconsidering the wisdom of the move when the cold air hit him. In the closet he found two extra blankets and put one over Laura.

The clock read three thirty-five. He wrapped the other blanket around himself and went to the window. Lights illuminated the state capitol, a gothic pile that looked more haunted mansion than seat of government. Taylor pitied poor old Albany. The provincial river town couldn't compete with a New York, not even a wounded, reeling one. People cared what happened to NYC. The world looked on in fascination when it burned or went broke. No one south of Poughkeepsie gave a shit about Albany.

To the right rose the near-completed new skyline commissioned by now Vice President Rockefeller. The filing-cabinet modernism of the Empire State Mall was like some fake future capital dreamed up for a World's Fair.

"What's out there?" Laura, wrapped in the blanket, pressed up to him.

"Rockefeller's folly. He blew millions."

"Can you see The Egg from here?"

"It's that blob to the right. They've been working on it since '66."

"My father says Rockefeller has an edifice complex. God, he hates that man."

"Does he *know* him?"

"Definitely. Nelson is a real disappointment to Daddy's wing of the Grand Old Party."

She moved around in front of him, opened her blanket, and closed it around them both. She was shivering.

"You're cold."

"Warm me up."

They went back to bed and made love again, slower this time but with more passion and less guesswork. He didn't fall asleep immediately after. Instead, he stared at the filigreed plaster of the ceiling and planned his next steps. He'd get going early to make Declan McNally's funeral and Joshua Harper's memorial service. He couldn't wait on Jansen anymore. If Voichek didn't show, he'd start talking to homeless people to get on the man's trail.

It was Saturday. The weekend would help. He had two clear days to make as much progress as possible on the McNally story *and* figure out what to tell Garfield and Worth about Joanna Kazka and her daughter. He followed the plaster paths in the ceiling as his mind tracked leads. He didn't know who Pickwick was, and what was worse, the man was now messing in matters that could destroy his career and get the Kazkas killed. Taylor didn't like being manipulated. His eyes stopped in a plaster cul-de-sac. What were the hidden connections that led from Joanna to those who set him up? That too was a dead end. He was either close to a breakthrough or he'd trapped himself. Which was it? He imagined charging headlong at a finish line that turned out to be a cliff. The cartoon image would be funny if so much weren't at stake.

He propped his head on the palm of his hand and watched Laura sleep for five minutes, ten, until his eyelids lowered in time with her breathing, and he dropped off.

17

-------◆-------

A T THE FRONT of St. Patrick's Cathedral, a deputy mayor spoke about Declan McNally. "I count myself a good friend of this incredible family struck by terrible tragedy. Here was a boy who was always willing to help those in need. No one worked harder in school than he did."

The students from Eli filled five pews across the aisle from Taylor. The girls were crying. The boys didn't know what to do with themselves. He was too far from the front to see the family, though for a moment he thought he glimpsed Lydia McNally's thick brown hair as she leaned on Constable's shoulder. Enough flowers to fill the Brooklyn Botanical surrounded the coffin. The cloud of incense floating around the casket masked their bouquet. The churchy, sweet odor of death.

The priest came last, his job to cap the proceedings with salvation. "We want him back. We are the lost ones."

The girls cried louder, and a moan came from the family up front. The boys shuffled their feet.

"We grieve for our loss. Declan is not lost. He is risen. Let us pray."

He followed the crowd down the aisle and stood on Fifth

Avenue at the edge of the large group. The wind whipped overcoats so they crackled in the wind like black flags. He moved toward Constable McNally, who was thanking people in a makeshift receiving line at the bottom of the cathedral steps.

Taylor reached the front. "My condolences, Mr. McNally."

"Call me Con." McNally moved back a couple of steps from the line. He fixed his clear blue eyes on Taylor. "I want to thank you, if I didn't properly Wednesday night. If it wasn't for you, we would never have found him."

"Looks like someone was trying to make your son disappear."

"I don't think so. They're incompetent at Bellevue. They weren't doing their goddamned jobs." He lowered his voice back into sadness. "We would still have been looking for our boy."

"No doubt the homicide detectives are very focused on the case." He left the obvious unspoken. The police will do it because Constable had been a cop and his father-in-law was Democratic Party chief.

"Yeah, they'll turn over heaven and earth. Cops always take care of their own. But their best isn't what it used to be. The NYPD is crippled."

The receiving line became clusters of people waiting for McNally to return. His wife bent her head to a gray-haired woman, who was weeping quietly.

"Listen, I will never forget it was you who ID'd our son. Not a cop. Certainly not the coroner. Please tell me, have you got anything new?"

"I'm tracking down some leads. I'll let you know what I find. It would help if I had an idea on suspects. Do you? Did Declan have enemies?"

"No. None. That's why this is so hard for us. He was a good kid, well liked by everyone. You must have heard that."

Taylor hadn't heard anything like that, except from the

girlfriend. An out-of-touch dad? Or was something else going on?

McNally rubbed the dark shadows under his eyes. "He got up to the usual teenage stuff. Nothing wrong with that. Especially at that school. You need to let them blow off steam."

"What about you? You can make a lot of enemies working as a cop."

"Me? It'd destroy me if someone did this to get at me." A weary shake of the head. "No one's ever threatened me. You know, 'I'll get you copper,' as he was being dragged off to jail. Demarco and Simone are checking my files."

"They can be a pain in the ass, but they get the bad guys."

"They haven't impressed me so far. They're also checking into threats against my father-in-law. There's somebody with enemies."

A heavyset man in a black suit came over to McNally and spoke to him in an undertaker's hushed tones. McNally again looked over at his wife, who was in the middle of the crowd now. Assistants loaded flowers into the back of the hearse, all but obscuring the coffin.

"Sorry, I have to talk to these people before we go. This day is never going to end. Call my office. I want to know how you're getting on." McNally walked off.

Yes, he'd call on Monday. He wasn't finished asking about enemies. He also had questions to ask McNally about his son's behavior. They weren't the kind for right after the funeral.

18

———◆———

TAYLOR STOOD BEHIND the last row of chairs in the cramped chapel of Morrison & Sons Funeral Home on West 47th. The room was filled with the homeless, plus some soup kitchen and social worker types, and AA people from the days when Joshua Harper was trying to get sober. They all came to remember the life of a homeless man who died outside the Akron Bus Station trying to get to his wife and kid in Topeka. The place smelled of closely packed bodies, booze, cigarettes, and wet carpet. A flat-faced man in an ill-fitting suit spoke for a good fifteen minutes over coughing and the rustling of coats.

"I know in my heart that Joshua continued to search for peace. Now let us recite the Serenity Prayer." That confirmed his AA credentials.

The group droned. "God, grant me the serenity to accept the things I cannot change, the courage to change the things I can, and the wisdom to know the difference."

The flat-faced man called for quiet contemplation.

An older man with a trimmed, snow-white beard and ruddy face squeezed in next to Taylor. "You're the reporter looking for me?" the man whispered. "I'm Voichek."

"Yes. We need to talk. You're being chased?"

"Had to see Joshua off, though." He was short and stocky, with a face that had a lot of stories to tell. He wore a fisherman's sweater, work pants flared at the bottom, and a wool, hound's-tooth overcoat. "Jansen thinks you can help."

"I'll try. Who's after you?"

"The guys who bought my clothes."

A woman sitting in the row in front of them turned and gave Taylor a look.

He lowered his voice. "The clothes Declan McNally had on?"

"I guess. From what I hear, at least. It's my jacket. I had no idea they were going to put my stuff on a dead kid. Hear me. I don't beg. I earn everything I spend. So when someone offers five dime notes for my clothes, I don't ask questions."

"Did you know the men?"

"Never seen them before. And I see a lot of people around this town." He turned to check the door. "Oh shit. That's them." Voichek stepped hard on Taylor's right foot as he squeezed past, jostled along the back of the tiny room toward the corner and up the right aisle to the front.

Three men in trench coats, one wearing a snap-brim fedora, the two others in black watch caps, pushed into the room from the main doorway, shouldering aside mourners. An old woman banged into the wall with a weak cry. The room was small. They would get to Voichek fast. Something needed to be done.

"Jansen, the men at the back of the room in trench coats," Taylor yelled. "Stop them for as long as you can."

Jansen popped up like a gopher. "Everyone. This is an emergency. Head to the back of the room. Now!"

A red-haired man in bib overalls, the first to move, tumbled to the floor, shoved by the man in the fedora. Rows emptied. People pushed to the back, forming a clot of bodies around the intruders. The sudden surge carried Taylor along toward the thugs even as he tried to hold his ground. He couldn't fight the press of bodies. Voichek was going for a doorway in the front corner of the chapel. Taylor couldn't lose him now; yet he was being pushed in the opposite direction.

He climbed onto the chair in front of him. With everyone standing, all the seats were empty. He ran down the row on the seats of the folding chairs, almost toppled over when one rickety seat flipped up, twisted his right ankle, jumped to the next one and made it to the aisle at the wall. His ankle screamed in pain. Voichek sprinted past Joshua Harper's urn. Taylor started hobbling up the aisle.

Someone behind yelled. The three men punched and pushed their way through the crowd at a far faster pace than Taylor would have hoped. Cries. Shouts at various volumes and pitches. The thugs threw people aside as if they were rag dolls.

One voice pleaded, "Don't step on Jerry. Get Jerry off the floor."

Voichek disappeared through the doorway. Fedora raised a large caliber revolver over his head and fired the gun into the ceiling. Survival instincts kicked in, and the homeless crouched to the ground as if a bomb had gone off.

Taylor made the doorway into the next room. The gunshot didn't freeze Voichek. He ran between two rows of caskets parked like cars in a lot. Each carried a card displaying a price in magic marker. They'd both found safety, if short lived, in Morrison & Sons' showroom. The gun went off again. Taylor's reflexes triggered. He dove sideways, slid off the top of a glossy maple casket and onto the floor next to a black one. He'd covered shootings daily for ten years, but he'd never been on the receiving end. Everything was happening too fast. Out of control. Chaos and pandemonium.

Voichek ran with the speed of a young man through the far door of the showroom. Taylor followed him into a workroom, forced his right ankle to take weight it had no interest in and went through a door to burst into the cold, mid-afternoon sunlight. He ran as best he could east on 47th. They were both easy targets now, and Taylor was the nearest. Voichek made the corner and took off up Ninth. Taylor picked up the pace, turned onto the avenue and leveled an old lady leaving a corner bodega with two shopping bags.

"Sorry, sorry." Navel oranges rolled around on the sidewalk. He got to his feet.

"Get away from me!"

"I'm sorry." He crossed 48th as Voichek climbed on an M9 bus. He urged one last bit of speed out of his heavy legs and pained right ankle and threw his arm between the closing doors of the bus. The doors shut on it.

"Ow! Open up."

"Man, there's other damn buses." The driver swung the handle to open them again.

Taylor limped to the backseat where Voichek crouched. Fedora ran toward the bus as it pulled away from the curb and turned on his heels to chase as the bus passed. He got alongside and banged at the door. He screamed at the driver.

Voichek yanked Taylor down onto the hard plastic seat with violent strength. "You don't need to make it easy for them."

"They saw you get on."

"Wouldn't have if you'd stayed the hell off."

"I'm tired of this," said the driver. "Why can't anyone wait for the next damn bus today?"

Taylor stood again and moved forward, prepared to tell any sort of story about the man to keep the bus moving. He was thrown back as the driver shifted up a gear and moved the bus into the middle of the avenue with a diesel roar. Fedora yelled once more and continued banging, the raps receding down the side of the bus and ceasing after a final bang on the rear.

"Would you please sit down?"

"Not till I know they aren't following us." Behind the bus, a black Oldsmobile stopped to pick up Fedora and sped forward. "Shit, they are."

Taylor sat back on the seat. Voichek looked determined

rather than frightened. Fear had tightened Taylor's chest at the instant the first shot had been fired. The tension spread to his entire body as he thought of that Oldsmobile, like he might remain frozen there until something bad happened. Unless he acted, the car would catch the bus and the men would jump on and grab Voichek. The bus stopped for a red light. Ahead, ramps arched into Port Authority Bus Terminal. These gave Taylor an idea. He tugged Voichek by the coat sleeve and urged him to the front of the bus. The Olds was stuck behind a police car at a red light one block back. "Don't Walk" signs already flashed on both sides of the avenue. The light would change any second. Taylor swung the handle and opened the bus door.

"Jesus man, what are you doing? I'm driving this bus."

Taylor didn't answer but pulled Voichek out into the middle of Ninth and urged him to run for the curb as the traffic light flicked to green. Cars jumped at the two of them like dogs on leashes and braked hard as the men ran past. Drivers swore. A bumper caught Taylor's right leg with enough force to knock him to the pavement. His bad right ankle blazed. He regained his feet and barely dodged between a car and a truck behind Voichek to make the sidewalk as the traffic took off. The police car peeled away east onto 41st, lights and siren on.

"Shit. Hoped the cops would stay around longer than that."

The Olds hit the gas and raced catty-corner across the avenue toward them.

Taylor maintained something like a limping trot west down 40th with Voichek beside him. Brakes squealed when the Olds tried to come down the one-way street the wrong way and jumped the curb to avoid a head-on. At least that part of the plan had worked. The three men would have to come on foot. Here was a race Taylor and Voichek needed to win.

"Where the hell are we going?"

Taylor didn't answer. He kept moving, grimacing, worrying that his ankle would seize up if he stopped. He swerved off the street onto a concrete roadway. They ran behind a bus from

Jersey as they rose up into the spider web of ramps that fed Port Authority from the Lincoln Tunnel and local streets. The diesel fumes stank and came close to choking Taylor as he sucked in air. Another bus pulled onto the ramp behind them. It might block any view of them from 40th. As long as they didn't get run over first. Taylor wasn't counting on anything, including the amount of time they had before the villains figured out where they went. They must disappear.

Another ramp spiraled next to the one they were on, separated by a two-foot gap and a long drop to the ground. Taylor climbed onto the concrete wall and signaled to Voichek to do the same. Taylor leaped to the other roadway and rolled into something a lot less elegant than a somersault as he tried to land using only his good leg. Voichek executed a graceful drop to the pavement, looked up and grabbed Taylor's right arm to haul him off the ground. Taylor flattened along the retaining wall as a commuter bus rolled down, horn blaring.

"Thanks."

"Wouldn't let you get run over, even if you are trying mighty hard to get yourself killed."

Taylor leaned over to look at the ramp they'd escaped. No sign of the bad guys. He started up the down-ramp along the side, buses passing within inches on their way to the Lincoln Tunnel, each driver blasting his horn to make sure they got the message they weren't supposed to be there.

"You go on ahead." Taylor pointed to the bus-sized door into the terminal. His limp was worse. "I'll slow you down."

"I don't leave anyone behind."

There was no time to argue. They kept on and made it into Port Authority. Taylor leaned back out to peer down the ramps. The three men jogged halfway up the first roadway. One looked up. Taylor ducked his head inside. Had he been seen?

He led the way past numbered gates, panting. The diesel fumes were even thicker here. On the main level, they saw no sign of the three men, just day visitors from Jersey. Taylor wanted to put distance between themselves and the three hoods. Somewhere safe, where he could talk to Voichek. They took the stairway to the subway. Voichek didn't have the fare, so Taylor flipped him a 35 cent token. They boarded the first uptown C train.

19

———◆———

A BUNDLE ON the street a few steps beyond the subway stairs spoke as they passed. "Hey, Voichek, still king of the road?"

"Whatever that road is, Pennyman." Voichek fished for change until he came up empty.

The bundle, with so little face showing the man could have been any age from twenty to sixty, sat in front of an upended Green Beret and cardboard sign. "Vet. Please. Help."

"Let's keep going." Taylor led them along 81st and up to the Lighthouse Coffee Shop at 84th and Broadway. A second—maybe third—cousin of Taylor's grandfather owned the place. He'd met the man once in his teens and didn't plan to announce his visit now. He wanted somewhere people wouldn't look for him. That ruled out the Oddity. He was sure they'd eat well at the Lighthouse. He'd been raised to trust in the kitchen of a Greek coffee shop.

Taylor walked to the door, ready for the warmth, a seat, and coffee rich with half-and-half and sugar. Voichek continued up the street.

"Where are you going?"

"I'm sorry. It was a mistake trying to meet. That's the closest they've come. I gotta stay away from those yeggs. They're shooting at people." He waved his hands in exaggerated fashion over his head, his fingers formed into pistols like a kid playing cowboys.

"Tell me what happened. If it's the truth, and you didn't know about Declan—"

"I don't lie. Not about anything. Why the hell should I sit with you when you're calling me a liar?"

"Sorry. No, I'm not." That was a mistake. Voichek needed to see him as an ally. "Talk to me about who bought your clothes. Maybe I can help."

"You got some kind of in with the bulls? They hear my story and they'll grab me for a stay in the calaboose. Those thugs know how to get at you on the inside."

"I'll keep it anonymous and figure out what is really going on. How else will you stop them from chasing you?"

"Maybe. I'll think about it."

Taylor spoke quickly before Voichek could walk off. "How have they stayed on your trail? They must know something about the places the homeless go."

"I'm *not* homeless. I'm a hobo. I choose to live this way. And I live well."

"They've tracked you for a week around the city. They know something. Doesn't that make sense?"

This seemed to hit a nerve. Voichek rubbed at his neat beard. The man had stayed clean and tidy while on the run. He was resourceful and proud.

"They don't know who I am," Taylor persisted. "Where I go. Who I know. If you work with me, maybe we can throw them off."

"I don't work with anyone for long." He looked down the block and wavered.

"Let me buy you dinner. Spend a half hour with me."

"I don't take charity either."

"Won't be charity. Tell me what you know. You'd be doing me a favor."

"That doesn't sound much like work."

"Believe me, it is. It's how the news gets covered in this city."

Taylor opened the door and held it for Voichek. The smell of fried comfort poured out into the cold. Eggs and hash, burgers and fries. Voichek nodded, apparently convinced this was the right move, at least for the moment.

The place was smaller than the Oddity, as everyone called his Grandpop's coffee shop, The Odysseus, on the Eastside. The Lighthouse had a counter on the right and small booths on the left. At the back beyond the counter were six larger booths. Without asking, Voichek took the last one and sat facing the front, after he'd peeked into the kitchen behind.

"How's it look?"

"There's a back door through a crowded kitchen. Go left, then straight out."

"You always check?"

"Always."

The Lighthouse didn't play up the Greek connection like The Odysseus. Cousin likely agreed with some members of the diner-owning fraternity who believed ethnic identity was a liability. Items from a seashore souvenir stand hung on the wall. A lobster trap, a couple of red plastic crabs, and three plaster lighthouses.

Taylor's right leg throbbed something terrible. He pulled up the pant leg. The ankle above his sock was swollen.

"That's ugly enough." Voichek crouched down from his chair and gave the ankle a gentle squeeze.

Taylor bit the inside of his lip to keep from yelling.

"Lucky for you, you probably just twisted it. Don't take your shoe off or you'll never get it back on."

"You're sure?"

"Life on the road and four years fighting taught me enough. Yeah, I'm sure."

"I'll be okay for now."

The table was chipped blue Formica, with menus in a black wire rack that also held sugar packets and salt and pepper. The first two pages of the menu offered a wide selection of seafood dinners, all fried, all no doubt straight from the freezer. Some diner traditions were upheld. At the back, a full page was dedicated to breakfast, plus a section with pot roast, meatloaf, and London broil.

In swift, practiced moves, a gray-haired waitress set down two glasses of tap water and two coffee cups, returned and filled the cups and put a steel pitcher of half and half on the table.

"I'll have Adam and Eve on a raft, eyes open," Voichek said.

"Hon, it's been an age since I heard that kinda order."

"It's hobo talk. Means eggs over—"

"Easy on toast. I know what it means. Just haven't heard it in such a long time. I worked a little lunch wagon out in Jersey when I was a kid. A lot of the customers were 'boes." She looked at Taylor. "What about you, hon?"

"Hash and eggs, eggs poached."

The waitress pushed open the kitchen door and yelled inside, "Get this one, Eddie. I got an order for Adam and Eve on a raft, eyes open. When did you hear that last?"

"Don't know. It's been twenty years. All disappeared."

"You made their night." Taylor sipped the coffee. The taste and warmth of it brought a little smile to his face. "Jansen said you don't travel anymore."

"I quit five years ago." Sadness sapped the confident energy out of his voice. "The traveling, that's everything to a hobo. It's freedom. Or was. New York was my jungle. That's what we call a summer rest stop. I always lined up good work here when I stayed over. Passing out fliers, odd jobs on construction sites. Sometimes wore a sandwich board in front of a new restaurant. The trains, well, the trains had been going away for years. Interstates and trucking took care of them. All the great roads died. Rolled up into that ugly mess Conrail. The Pennsy, gone. Less Sleep and More Speed, the Lake Shore and Michigan Southern, gone. All gone. The Mullet Line. The Original Ham and Egg Route. All Tramps Sent Free. I could tell you their real names, but you wouldn't know them. They're gone and forgotten. You can't hop a freight when the boxcars are all locked up. So I stayed here. I'm home-guard. Someone who leaves the road. I'm still a hobo. Still follow the code. Not a bum, not a tramp."

"What's the difference?"

"A hobo is someone who travels to work." Voichek's eyes flashed a challenge. "A tramp is someone who travels and won't work. A bum is someone who won't travel and won't work. You've got a lotta damn bums in this town."

"How many of you are still around?"

"God only knows. There's hardly anyone on the road anymore. I feel like someone whose language is dying. You know, like the Indian in *The Last of the Mohicans*. I figure if I don't use the words, the language will die completely."

Here was a different sort of death. No investigation. No story. Not even an obituary. Voichek's hobo language would disappear without any notice whatsoever.

"Maybe I can get a story on your lingo in the *MT*."

"Why?"

"I like words. I mean, they're my job." Taylor shrugged. "It's not the sort of story I usually do. I bet I can find someone at the paper who will."

Laura, in fact. She had a talent for features. She'd even taken some linguistics courses at Columbia. He'd scoffed at those classes six months ago. Sometimes he could be a real idiot. He'd make up for that mistake by pointing her to this story.

"Jansen says you write the obits."

"That *was* what I did."

When the food came, Voichek dug in like he hadn't seen food in days, which was more than likely. Taylor let the man have his meal. His own smelled glorious and set his stomach rumbling. He stabbed the eggs so the yellow yoke mixed with the corn beef hash and ate quietly and almost as quickly. No wonder. He'd last eaten at six that morning, when he and Laura picked up coffees and hard rolls on the way out of Albany.

"I needed that. Thank you."

"So did I."

Voichek's eyes widened. "Goddamn it. Those yeggs again!"

He bolted out of the booth and through the kitchen door. It swung back and forth, the only sign he'd been there. Taylor turned. Fedora and one of the other two thugs stood at the front of the coffee shop. *How the hell did they find us?* He ran after Voichek and caught him before he could pull open the back door.

"Don't. There's only two of them. The third may have the back covered."

"We're trapped in this stew pot."

Taylor turned to the bewildered cook. "My grandfather owns the Odysseus on Madison. He's cousins with your boss. There are guys after us out front. Probably out back too. Is there another way out of here?"

"You're cousins with me, cousin." The cook spoke in accented English. He slammed home the dead bolt on the back door. "You're still trapped bad."

The wiry, olive-skinned man looked at the way into the restaurant and at the back door. He waved his hand like he had the answer, stepped into a little nook around the corner from the stove, threw brooms and mops out of the way and opened a closet door. "This way."

Voichek looked in first. "Hide in a storage room? We're walking into a cage."

"No, see the floor. You go down to the basement to get to the front of the building. Go quick. They'll figure it out soon enough."

Voichek reached down and found an iron ring. He pulled

open the trapdoor and dropped down into the black hole without looking back.

Taylor turned to his distant cousin. "What are you going to do?"

"Make sure no one's hurting my dad."

"They're armed."

"Cast iron's a pretty good weapon too."

With a determined smile, he disappeared around the corner. Taylor swung into the hole, his feet on a steep stairway—more a ladder posing as one—and descended, leaning on the right leg as little as possible. He eased the trapdoor closed.

Voichek moved quickly through the cluttered basement toward the front of the building. Taylor stepped off the bottom stair, stifled a yell as his twisted right ankle flared, and hobbled to where Voichek had stopped. The hobo looked up a steel ramp of rollers that sloped toward a pair of doors. This was the route supplies took into the Lighthouse's basement through the iron trap door in the sidewalk above. It was their only way out.

"We gotta get up it fast. And that doesn't look easy." Voichek grabbed the edges of the ramp. "They'll sure as hell catch us down here. Never go down a dead end."

He moved, using the outside frame to avoid the rollers. His shoulder knocked the basement's single exposed light bulb as he climbed. It swung in a violent loop, turning the shadows of crates and shelves into mountains, then miniatures in wild shifts. Taylor followed, and because he was looking down to mind his footing, heard rather than saw Voichek slide the bolt and grunt as he put his shoulder to one of the two iron doors.

A crash from somewhere above, maybe the kitchen.

Taylor reached the top. He moved his right leg completely off the loading ramp because there wasn't room for both men and the leg wouldn't be any use in pushing. Voichek hadn't shifted the door an inch. "Together."

They both hunched their shoulders against it, and the metal

door began to creak up and out. Looking back through his legs again, Taylor saw a square of light appear in the basement ceiling. They heaved again. The door swung wide and slammed against the pavement with a crash.

"We've got them!" said a voice from the trapdoor. "Jo-Jo, down now."

Taylor missed his footing and instinctively tried to catch hold with his right leg. Pain shot up through his ankle. He fell over the side of the ramp and grabbed the metal with his left hand just in time to stop from dropping eight feet to the cartons and concrete below. Everyone moved but him. Voichek up and out into the light, and one of the thugs quickly down the ladder into the basement. He swung by one hand for several long seconds, thought his grip was going to give, somehow got his right hand on the ramp; finally, stretching his left leg to hook a heel, he pulled himself up and scrambled toward blue sky. A hand reached in.

"Let's go. I've no intention of taking the Westbound tonight. Not at the hands of these damn villains." Voichek pulled just as Taylor's footing slipped. He slid backward on the rollers, threatening to drag both of them down to their pursuers. Voichek slammed a battered shoe against the lip of the door to stop Taylor. He gave a hard yank. They both fell over onto the sidewalk. A flash of light and a crack. A second flash-crack. Gun shots in the basement.

"Let's move." Voichek took off. Taylor followed. An old man in an apron came out of the door yelling at the two of them in Greek. That was bad; Greek was always a terrible sign with relatives. Grandpop was going to get a phone call. Taylor moved as fast as he could down Broadway behind Voichek, crossing traffic mid-block and dodging a honking car. Voichek slowed down to wait at 83rd.

"We need to get somewhere you can rest that leg. Maybe get it wrapped."

"I know."

Taylor led them to Central Park West and back down to the 81st Street subway station.

"Why the hell are we coming back here?" Voichek stopped and looked around.

"I need to check something." Taylor hurried over to the spot next to the subway stairs. He kicked over the coffee cup. Sludge and swollen cigarette butts spilled on the ground, flakes of tobacco swirling on the surface of the liquid. The cardboard sign remained. He bent down and picked up two dimes and three pennies. Why would a beggar leave any money behind? Where's your friend Pennyman?"

"I don't know. Why does it matter?"

"Is this his usual spot?"

"Yeah. He likes the folks who live in the apartment buildings on the park. He's been working them a long while."

"Would he quit this early?"

"Doubt it. Still lots of daylight."

"Those men didn't follow us to the coffee shop. They weren't inside Port Authority. They weren't on the subway. I was too careful. So how the hell did they find us? From the time we escaped the funeral parlor, Pennyman was the only person I heard ID you. They must have homeless people on the lookout for you. A bounty maybe. There's no other way they could have known where we went. That's how they've stayed on you all week."

Instead of going into the subway, Taylor warily walked down to 72nd and west to Amsterdam. They passed the Gray's Papaya at the corner, took the stairs to the Broadway Local, and rode three stops north.

At 3:45, Taylor used a pay phone on the platform to leave a message for Harry Jansen. They got back on and rode under Manhattan, switching trains in a random tour of the subway lines that crisscrossed under the island. Moving was the safest way to hide until Jansen responded. Voichek dozed off on one long stretch from Harlem to Wall Street. Taylor might have wished for sleep, but the throbbing in his right leg kept a painful drumbeat. That made it easy to stay awake and watch for anyone who recognized Voichek. He wouldn't let his guard down again.

20

———◆———

TAYLOR HUNG UP the phone and stepped over to where Voichek leaned against a pillar on the N platform in Union Square station. The man looked ready to bolt. Here was a guy who set his own rules and routes. He wasn't going to put up with Taylor for long. This news wasn't going to help either.

"The guys chasing you are offering money to street people. Twenty dollar bounty to report your location. Fifty on top if you're caught. Pennyman must have taken their money."

"Bums and drunks." Voichek spit out the words.

"Jansen got a couple of people to admit it's been going on for a week. They were afraid to tell him."

"Because they want to collect."

"That's our biggest problem now. We don't know who will head for a pay phone as soon as they see you."

"It's *my* problem. I'll solve it by staying away from every bum, tramp, and lowdown drunk in this town. I'll leave. I haven't forgotten how to make it on the road."

"You can't just run away. You're the only person who can tie those men to your clothes. Those clothes tie them to the murder of a teenage boy. That's why they're trying to kill you."

"Seems the only thing I can do." Voichek still leaned against the pillar, looking pensive. An N train to Coney Island pulled in. "Let's go."

Taylor knew it was now or never. The story wasn't adding up. Why buy Voichek's clothes and only later try to kill him? He was holding something back, and Taylor had to find out what it was. They sat opposite each other in the nearly empty car. "Tell me what happened with your clothes."

"The leader—the one with the scar on his face—did all the talking. The other two just stood there. The fatheaded one smoked a cigar. The leader didn't say much. Just how much he'd pay. I didn't ask anything. When someone offers silly money, the less said the better. I didn't know they were going to dress the kid in them. Or whatever they did. I didn't know they were going to make my life miserable."

"Killing you is a bit more than misery."

"The Germans tried harder."

"They paid you fifty?"

"Yes. That's a lot of money for me. A real lot."

"I have no doubt, but you're not telling me the whole story."

"You're calling me a liar again?" Voichek turned angry in an instant, like a switch had flipped. He moved to the door. "You don't know me for more than a few hours and you call me a liar twice. Where do you get off?"

"This Army field jacket." Taylor tugged at his collar. "My brother gave it to me before he left for Vietnam for the last time. I wouldn't sell this jacket to anyone. How about yours? Jansen told me you wore it through World War II. Sewed the flags of the world on it because you believed—I guess everybody believed once—that war won a special peace. You never took it off. I don't see you parting with that jacket. I find it hard to believe the guys chasing us—"

"*Me.* They're chasing me."

"Fine—the guys chasing you are the type who buy things

from homeless people. And what? Only later decide to murder them? None of it makes sense."

"I'm a hobo, not homeless. I've got some honor left." His voice was quiet and he looked down. The train braked into Utrecht Avenue, raising a banshee racket. People on the platform put their hands to their ears to block out the noise. The cars stopped with a sharp jolt. Voichek stood at the doorway. If the man were leaving, he'd do it now. He stayed where he was as the doors rattled open and closed and did it again. After a half-dozen bangs, the doors stayed shut and the conductor signaled with two buzzes for the driver to pull out. Voichek sighed, rubbed his ears as if they were cold but in a rough way that looked like it hurt. He sat. "It's embarrassing. Is that what you reporters do? Figure out what's really embarrassing for someone and tell the world?"

"What I want to do is tell the world who murdered Declan McNally. Who made it look like he froze to death on the street. Who did that and why. When I do, whoever is involved will be a whole lot more than embarrassed."

"I've never been rolled. The Great Depression, thousands and thousands of miles on the tracks, hobo camps all over this land, a world war, and years in this city. Nobody has ever rolled me till those three hijackers. It was Monday evening, freezing cold and already getting dark. I'm walking down an alley off of West 46th. Out of nowhere, two of them are at one end and one at the other. I'm trapped. I tell them I don't have anything worth their time. 'Take off your clothes,' says the one with the scar. He hits me hard in the gut. 'Worthless fucking street scum. You're not even worth what you're wearing. I hate your kind.' One of the others points a gun. They'd all been drinking. I could tell from their talk and their smell. I start undressing in that freezing wind. Everything's off but my pants. I pull them down slowly. Just as they're off my feet, I use the belt to whip the pants straight at the face of the one with the gun. I run the other way fast as I can. I put my shoulder into the gut of the yegg blocking the end of the alley. He yells, surprised-like. I guess he didn't expect a good smack from some old geezer. I run to 45th, hear a shot. Think I did at least. That just makes me go faster. I'm running in my longjohns down the street. Embarrassing. Funny, like in a movie, if they weren't trying to kill me for my clothes. I'm convinced they're going to get me. Or the cops will. Or the cold will. I get to the corner at Ninth and see another guy from Jansen's shelter, name of Wiley. I beg him to let me borrow his trench coat for ten minutes. He's a bit of a tramp, but a good egg and lets me. He waits inside a deli with a cup of coffee and a sandwich I buy him."

Taylor glanced up from the notebook.

"I keep my cash in my sock. I go into Ben Franklin's, grab the first warm clothes I see and put them on in the dressing room. Wiley's trench coat is back over top. I'm a buck short at the register for the gear, so I'm running again. I'd never lifted before. Not ever. A hobo doesn't thieve. That will get you buried deep in the coop."

"The coop? Jail?"

"A long damn time in jail. You lose your freedom, you lose the most important thing you have. Now you know the truth. Those three would have killed me. I'm sure of it. They're trying to kill me now."

"They were going to murder you for your clothes?"

"People die every day for less. No one cares. A guy gets killed for a bottle of cheap wine or a loaded syringe. They'd kill me and dump me somewhere and nothing would happen. C'mon, it's the same reason they wanted my clothes. They wanted to turn the dead kid invisible. We're all invisible." Voichek slumped on the bench, deflated. "Now every vagrant and bum is trying to sell me out. This can't get any worse."

He was right on one count. Dozens of homeless people died every month. No one took notice. No one tried to figure out what happened at the end of each of those lives. Taylor had to work his ass off to get the killing of a single homeless man in the paper. He didn't need to do a thing when the well-off bought it. The story wrote itself. Hell, it published itself.

"Jansen said he can guarantee most of his people."

"Most?" A sad laugh. "Jansen's all right. He puts a roof over all of them. So, what are they going to tell him? There are drunks there, dope fiends and criminals too stupid to figure out what to steal. A whole bunch that would turn me in for the money."

They sat in silence for three stops. Every time the train made the same earsplitting squeal before braking to a stop. The subway map across from Taylor gave him an idea. He followed the N line to its end. "There aren't many homeless people out on Coney Island, are there?"

"Not this time of year. No shelters. No one to beg off. It's a long way out of town. And even colder."

"That may be just the place for us. For a while, at least."

Voichek didn't react, instead stared out his window at Brooklyn passing below. The subway turned into an El six stops ago, rising out of the ground to ride on tracks above the streets and houses. The neighborhoods looked almost like the suburbs, with brick houses and tiny, snow-covered backyards lining quiet streets.

"I'm going to help you because they killed the kid," Voichek said after the noise of another stop. "Don't take too long with what you need to do. I don't want to end up dead too."

Taylor didn't have a reassuring answer for that, so he kept quiet. He was tired of being banged around by subway trains. His ankle hurt and the rest of his body was sore. He wanted off, wanted to sit still and think about the story taking shape. The local took a long forty minutes to get all the way to the end of the line. He pulled himself up as soon as the train stopped at Stillwell Avenue, went through the door and kept walking. Even now, holding onto a guy like Voichek would be like trying to grab smoke. He'd follow or he wouldn't. The cops had it so damn easy. Arrest, search, interrogate. Throw a guy in a cell. Soften him up. Question some more. They ought to be embarrassed every time he reported what they couldn't get. Nobody ever had to stop and answer his questions.

He clacked through the turnstile, Voichek right behind him. They both went down the stairs to the exit.

Across Surf Avenue was Nathan's Famous, with its truly famous block-long yellow sign. Neon promised seafood, buffet catering, French fries, cola and root beer, and of course, hot dogs.

"Not often I get to the seaside," Voichek said.

"That surprises me, with all your traveling."

"The road always ends at the sea. I don't like being at the end of the road. Told you, never go down a dead end."

Taylor pulled open the door. The restaurant was more crowded than he expected for a winter day. Then again, some people wouldn't eat a hot dog unless they got it from this old place. "Hungry?"

"Seems a long while since we were in that coffee shop."

"We've been riding for hours. Get whatever you want."

"Not charity, right? Because I'm helping you out."

"This is how journalism works."

Voichek smiled for the first time in almost four hours and ordered two hot dogs, one plain, one with fried onions, plus a dozen clams on the half shell and a coffee. Taylor added one with kraut and a glass of Pabst Blue Ribbon for his leg. They sat at one of three empty tables. The customers in the restaurant seemed no threat. One guy in the corner might be a vagrant or just working poor. He hadn't taken any notice of Voichek, who attacked the clams, slurping them with white horseradish.

"Cold and raw in the winter?"

"I eat them when I can get them. I'm not likely to get them again anytime soon."

Taylor took a bite of his dog, had a long draft of the beer, and decided it was pretty close to the best he'd ever tasted. He finished it quickly and got up to order another. Emergencies meant abandoning his rules.

"Would you mind getting me some fries?"

"Sure thing."

Taylor smiled at the old man's capacity to put it away. The hobo knew to eat for the days when he saw no food. He sat back down and sipped the second beer.

Voichek speared a French fry with one of those little wooden forks you only got at Nathan's. "I knew a hobo who worked for Nathan Handwerker."

"Who?"

"Who? You're the guy who's supposed to know everything about the city. *The* Nathan Handwerker who started this place. Before the war, Handwerker was having a hard time convincing people to stop here because of nicer sit-down joints all along the avenue. So he hires some hobos. He has them dress up like doctors and stand around in front of the place with signs on. 'If doctors eat our hot dogs, you know they're good!' "

"Guess it worked. Nathan's is *famous*. The other places are gone."

Taylor checked his ankle. The swelling hadn't gone down much.

"You'll probably live. If it were really bad, you wouldn't be walking."

"I'm prescribing Dr. Pabst's healing elixir." Taylor toasted with the beer glass. "Let me hear some more of that hobo language of yours."

Voichek sipped the steaming black coffee and smiled a second time. "You want me to *talk west*? That's what we call the lingo. Talking west."

"You named some of the trains." Taylor opened his notebook.

"They're called roads, not trains. Roads. The Big G is the Great Northern. The Bitter Biscuit Line, the Piedmont Division of the Southern. Only rode that once. Canned Meat & Stale Punk, the Chicago, Milwaukee & St. Paul. Damn Rotten Grub, the Denver and Rio Grande."

Taylor wrote them down. He couldn't wait to tell Laura

about the language. Once the story ran, it would go into Mrs. Wiggins' manila envelopes, in the bound volumes at the end of the year and even on microfilm at the Library of Congress. The great archiving machine couldn't help itself. Voichek's *talking west* would be saved forever. At least Taylor's version of forever.

"Accommodation is a local freight. A side-door Pullman, that's your basic boxcar. 'Course even the words that make up the language don't get used anymore. Do you know what a Pullman was, young man?"

"Sure, a sleeping car."

"Oh the things that have gone to ruin." Voichek shook his head. "A Pullman is far more than that. A Pullman sleeper on an express train was the most civilized form of travel there ever was on this earth. I rode one twice as a paying customer. Streaking across the country. With my private sitting room and pull-down bed. A Pullman porter waiting on me the whole time. Most of my life, a boxcar was my side-door Pullman."

"I thought hobos rode underneath freight trains."

"That's sleeping the gunnels, which is done by a *trapeze artist*. You had to be brave and more than a little crazy for that. The possum belly under a passenger car was okay though. Food, now we had lots of words for food because we were chasing meals whenever we weren't chasing rides. A combo was a dinner that didn't need cooking. The exhibition meal was grub you ate on the doorstep so the neighbors could appreciate the generosity of the lady of the house. Can you imagine that happening in this day and age? Anyone anywhere handing out food and wanting the neighbors to see a hobo eating on their front steps? We've gotten so civilized. No Pullmans. No exhibition meals." Voichek finished off the fries. "Here's one I haven't used in a long while. *Bridger*. I won't make you guess. It's someone who's ridden both steam trains and diesels. Someone who bridged the railroading eras. I'm a bridger, just. Can't be many of us left. Dying, like the language." He finished the coffee.

Taylor wrote *bridger* in his notebook and underlined it twice. There was Laura's lead. "Your language is going to be brand new to a lot of people. The only thing they know about hobos is Freddy the Freeloader on *The Red Skelton Show*."

"Don't write it until the killers are caught. I'm known for talking west out on the street. We don't need to give those yeggs any help. I'd like it if a story did some good. All's I see anymore are blank looks when I use words everyone around me used to know. There's no one to look out for you anymore. You could trust most people in a hobo jungle."

Taylor had the taste for a third beer but ruled it out because he had to keep his head clear. He ordered them both coffees and dumped sugar and half-and-half in his.

"You making dessert?" Voichek chuckled over his.

"How can you drink yours so hot?"

"Only way, over a campfire. Get to like it that way. Rarely any creamer around."

The caffeine and sugar gave Taylor an up-all-night tingle over the top of his two-beer buzz. He was all jitters and no focus. Exhaustion seeped into his bones. Time to get some work done before he crashed completely. He stretched and limped to the phone booth. He called Laura's apartment. Her roommate Sarah Jane said Laura wasn't around and did a bad job of acting like she was taking a message. A male voice yelled for Sarah Jane to come back to bed. He left a second message for Laura with the paper's weekend switchboard operator. He hung up and stood in front of the phone alone, and all of a sudden, lonely. He missed Laura. Albany might have been a week ago instead of last night. This day stretched out so long. He wanted her to be here so they could go over everything. He trusted her. She'd help think it through and that would ease his anxiety. He called Jansen's pay phone.

"It's gotten worse since we last talked."

"How's that possible?"

"Those mobsters are shaking my people down. It's no longer

the carrot. All stick. They know who you are by name."

"How?"

"You made yourself pretty famous when you chased the Street Sweepers away from the shelter. Then you got Joshua Harper back for his funeral. The homeless don't get much, so you don't have to do much for them to become a name on the street. My people are tough, but they're not *tough guys*. When they get knocked around enough, they tell what they know and sometimes make up things they don't. Whoever these mobsters are, they know your name and they know you're a *Messenger-Telegram* man chasing a story."

"Dammit. Listen, if you hear anything I should know—I mean anything—leave a message with the paper's switchboard. Anytime, day or night. Don't wait till we can talk."

"I understand."

"Were your people hurt?"

"Beat up pretty badly."

"Will they talk to me?"

"I don't know. They're all scared. I'll see what I can do. Take care of yourself. And please take care of Voichek."

"I think he can take care of himself."

"It's been a long time since he was in trouble this deep. I'm worried for both of you. This is getting very ugly. Violent and ugly."

Taylor was left with the question of how to tell Voichek they were in deeper jeopardy. He couldn't think of a good way and so put off worrying the old man with it and walked back to the table. Voichek was reading a *Daily News* left by two men who'd sat at the next table.

The ambush at the Lighthouse made Taylor hinky. He was more determined than ever to work the story now he knew that the mobsters stole Voichek's clothing. They were trying to kill Voichek to cover their tracks because they murdered Declan McNally. That had to be it. He couldn't do much sitting in Nathan's. Still, Coney Island was a safe haven. Out past the boardwalk was the ocean and Staten Island. After that, the Verrazano Narrows and Europe. Wouldn't hurt to rest here a bit longer. He wasn't sure what to do with Voichek. He couldn't keep the man safe by himself. Maybe an idea would come to him. He reached over to the neighboring table for another discarded paper, Friday's edition of the weekly *Brooklyn Bulletin*. He flipped to the police blotter, his favorite column in any of the dozens of weeklies that covered New York's neighborhoods.

PARK SLOPE—A 31-year-old thought she fought off two attackers after they grabbed her purse. The muggers jumped the woman at 10:17 p.m. on Fifth Avenue and pushed the victim to the sidewalk. She refused to let go after one grabbed her purse, and both men gave up, fleeing toward Fourth. Ten minutes later, one returned and stabbed her.

BROOKLYN HEIGHTS—A pickpocket team continued to plague the neighborhood. A 45-year-old woman lost her wallet to a "bump and run" while shopping in the A&P Supermarket on Henry Street.

WILLIAMSBURG—A mugger attacked three victims on the J-train, stealing cash and credit cards in a 12-hour robbery spree. A 6-foot-7, 230-pound man threatened to throw a 66-year-old woman on the tracks at Hewes Street if she didn't turn over her purse. He fled with it. Two hours later, at the same station, a man of the same description punched a man in the face and took his wallet. A third victim was accosted on a train traveling between subway stations.

CARROL GARDENS—A couple on a motor scooter chased down a thief who'd grabbed a woman's prize-winning poodle. The victim told police she was walking Pinkie's Powderpuff Pozo near Degraw and Hoyt when a teenager ran over and took the dog, whipping the leash out of her hand. The couple on the scooter gave chase. The woman rider hopped off and snatched Pinkie and jumped back on the scooter.

The blotter always had a dog story. He'd read the blotters enough in the past ten years to know the character of the crime had changed. More muggings. More murders. The subway was a great source of danger. He looked over the rest of the paper and traded with Voichek. He spent a while puzzling over a story about the Urban Development Corporation defaulting last month on $100 million in bonds. The writer was worried about New York City's debt and the fact it never actually got repaid. Six billion dollars sounded like a lot, but Taylor wasn't a numbers guy.

A uniformed Nathan's employee turned over chairs and put them on the tables. The wall clock read eleven-twenty. Time to head to Queens.

PART VI:
Sunday, March 16,
1975

21

———◆———

THEY'D CAUGHT THEIR first piece of good luck all day. A gypsy cab, red bandana tied around its whip antenna, pulled over after they'd stood on Stillwell for only ten minutes. The Chevy Bel Air's backseat was big enough to be a bed. Taylor would have happily stretched right across it to rest his throbbing right ankle if Voichek weren't along. Instead, he got as comfortable as he could. Brooklyn turned into Queens as the driver took local streets to Ahab's Bar & Grill.

Taylor handed the driver five bucks. An obscene amount, but obscene was the going rate for travel between outer boroughs at that time of night.

Inside Ahab's, Danny was impassive behind the bar and would be until last call at 4 a.m. and right through the lock-in for the hardcore drinkers at six. Voichek ordered rye on the rocks, Taylor a Rolling Rock pony. Danny, without being asked, picked up the black phone from below the bar and put it in front of Taylor. He was in his office away from the office. He was comfortable here, happy even.

Voichek lifted his drink. "Thanks for the third rail."

"Talking west?" Taylor clinked his bottle against the glass.

"Yeah. What we call booze."

Taylor dialed the *MT's* switchboard and picked up two messages from Laura, the last simply, "Call me. I'm worried."

The operator scolded him. "You need to get back to her."

Laura answered on the first ring.

So did her roommate. "Who's this?"

"Get off the damn phone, Sarah Jane! Are you okay? I've been worried to death."

"Don't need to be so testy." The phone clicked.

He took in a breath.

"I'm here still." Laura's warm voice was a tonic after the long hard Saturday. "Tell me everything."

"Man, there's so much. I'll start at the beginning. The McNally funeral was the full St. Pat's production. There must have been five hundred people. I talked with Constable McNally a little bit afterwards. I'm going to see him Monday. The fun really started at the service for Joshua Harper."

Voichek finished his whiskey. Taylor signaled Danny for another round and shifted a couple of barstools over to get privacy. Danny asked Voichek how he knew "the crazy reporter" and Voichek laughed.

In a low voice and leaving out no details, Taylor talked Laura through the Harper service, the chase, the Lighthouse ambush, the hours on the subway, Voichek's revelation he'd been robbed of his clothes and their time at Nathan's.

"Christ. Are you hurt?"

"Banged up a little." He drank the second beer. Each one tasted better. It would be a delicate balance numbing his ankle while keeping his head straight. Or straight enough.

"Do you want me to come out there?"

"No." He answered too fast. "I don't want you in danger."

"I'm not worried."

"The killers know who I am. I don't have a plan for what I'm going to do."

"About Voichek?" she guessed.

"Yes. Let's meet tomorrow afternoon. I need some sleep."

"At the *MT*?"

"Nah, not on Sunday. How about your apartment?"

"I like the way that sounds."

"As long as I'm sure no one's following. I'll call you either way. We still need to confirm that Declan was dealing up at Columbia. Find out who supplied him." He looked down the bar. "I should get back to Voichek." He didn't want to hang up.

"Take care of yourself."

"Don't worry. I'm no hero. Just a scribbler with a sore leg and a headache."

He missed her voice as soon as it was gone. Having her come over would have been the best thing in the world tonight. Laughter. Talk. Her touch. And a very bad idea. Voichek sipped the rye with an expression of relish that was surprising given the old man insisted on the cheapest brand in the rail. Voichek was his responsibility, and he had to see this through. He walked to the bathroom, turning over what to do next. He kept coming up with the same answer. Voichek wasn't going to like it. He was going to think Taylor was pushing him off after getting what he needed. No matter how it looked, it was time to talk to the cops. He returned to the bar with his mind made up "What we should …."

Voichek wasn't there. Danny hadn't seen him go. A note was scrawled on a cocktail napkin.

> I'm not one who can accept such hospitality without being able to repay. I appreciate what you're trying to do. There are yeggs and bulls everywhere in this mess. I'm better off alone. If I can think of anything that will help, I'll let you know. Please don't follow. I've told you everything I know but this: one of them said to the other, "This is a stupid reason for a contract." I assumed the contract was on me. Then I ran hard. Guess they really meant the kid. I'm going to keep running.
> —MV

"Shit, damn, shit."

Taylor stuffed the napkin in his pocket, waved at Danny to put the drinks on his tab and hobbled up and down the blocks around Ahab's. Back in front of the bar, he blew out vapor like an old steam engine. Voichek, the only thing close to a witness in the murder, had disappeared into the vastness of a New York City night. The man was at the mercy of any street person who'd take 20 dollars to tip the men trying to kill him. Worse. The bad guys were beating up homeless people to get information. He hadn't told Voichek about that development. It was going to be part of his speech on why they needed to go to the homicide cops. Voichek didn't understand the threat he faced, and it was Taylor's fault.

He needed to check the subway station next. He ran to the corner just as the black Oldsmobile sped past and skidded into a pool of blue and yellow light thrown by a store across the intersection. Fedora came out of the car.

Taylor didn't watch for the other two thugs, instead he ducked back into the bar. How'd they find him so goddamn fast? *Wait. Think about it.* The switchboard gave out Ahab's number to anyone after-hours. *Stupid.* He'd expected the thugs to keep searching Voichek's world on the street, not come directly after him. He'd been too tired to think straight and stupid to believe it would be safe here.

"Danny, you've got some villains behind me."

"Why are the bad guys always after you?"

"Autographs. They love what I write. Just don't say anything about me or my friend. You going to be okay?"

"Hunky dory."

Danny pulled an M1 rifle, his father's World War II original, from below the bar and rested it on the brown wood. Taylor watched from the dark back hall. The little pistol was strapped to his left ankle. He wasn't going to leave Danny in the lurch, not if things got ugly. The three men entered the front door and pulled up short. Of all the guns they might face in New

York City, this was near one of a kind. Fedora moved his hand up his coat.

Danny stroked the rifle. "Bub, this will blow such a big hole in you. Why, I'll be able to see your buddies shitting themselves behind."

"We were just looking for drinks." A distinct Italian accent. "Not a very friendly place you run, my friend."

"What you're looking for is the door. I've already called the cops."

"What are they going to say about that?" Fedora nodded at the rifle.

Danny shrugged. "They never seem to notice it when they get here."

The three men backed up, trying their best to look coolly unhurried as they retreated. Taylor left by the rear door and edged along the brick wall to the front corner of the building. The men studied the bar, as if figuring the strategy for a second assault.

Fedora pointed to the car. "We'll go to his house."

Shit. This was all going to hell. Taylor took a back way, came down a driveway across the street. As expected, the Oldsmobile was parked at his address. He eased between a retaining wall and the Moscowitz's Ford Falcon.

"Who could live here?" Fedora stood between the other two in Taylor's front yard. "The whole place is burned up. Burned and boarded up."

"This *is* the address." The one on the left walked over and peered into the trailer in the driveway, kicked open the door and went inside. "Looks like he lives here."

"What is he, some kinda fucking gypsy?"

The light flicked on and shadows danced across the windows of the little round Airstream. Things fell. One crash followed by another. They weren't being gentle with his stuff. Taylor knew they'd find nothing pawing through the remains of his life but was angered they'd wreck what little home he had. He limped to a pay phone a block away, called in a B&E and snuck back to the driveway. The thugs were in the Oldsmobile, parked a hundred feet up the block, the car dark but for the burning embers of cigarettes.

The Olds took off the instant the squad car's lights showed blocks away. The patrolmen spoke to Taylor for thirty seconds and went after it. The chase was always better than taking a statement from a pissed-off citizen. They came back twenty minutes later to get his description of the car and the men. Taylor said nothing of Voichek or the McNally murder.

He returned to Ahab's on the theory the villains wouldn't revisit the scene the same night. He drank ponies until his ankle went numb and kept going until it didn't feel like he had a leg. He was in a bittersweet mood, celebrating the break in the story, and at the same time unhappy that Voichek had left. He'd gotten good information from the old man but couldn't write a story connecting the clothes to the murder until he knew for certain where Voichek was. He'd never again file a story when the key source couldn't be located. Once burned and all that. Tinker Bell had taught him that a great deal of paranoia was a basic requirement. He waved for another beer. The three thugs were the key. He had to find out who they were and why they murdered Declan McNally.

22

———◆———

B Y UNIVERSAL JOURNALISTIC agreement, Sunday was the no-news day. Unless something large crashed, or a whole lot of people died in one place—or even better, both happened at the same time—most reporters didn't work. The paper's floors in the New Haven Life Insurance Company Building were empty but for a handful of weekend editors and the guys in sports.

Taylor, alone in the morgue, read a story on page 18 of the *New York Times*. South Vietnamese President Thieu ordered his troops to abandon the Central Highlands. South Vietnam retreated in the face of the oncoming forces from the North. The Sunday *Messenger-Telegram* hadn't even bothered with the wire copy. The few remaining dominos were falling. His brother hadn't sacrificed his life; he'd thrown it away. Taylor balled the paper up and threw it across the room. He wanted to hit something, hard. Damn, what did you do with anger when there was no one to take the blame? He held his head in his hands. He didn't have time for this. This was his last day on the McNally murder. Half the weekend was gone. He had good information on the stolen clothing, nothing on three nameless mobsters, and no Voichek. Come Monday, that wouldn't be enough. He liked Voichek and didn't want him to end up dead. How to stop it?

The door opened and Mrs. Wiggins came in. "You're more dedicated now than when you had a real job at this paper."

"What are you doing here?"

"I work here."

"On Sundays?"

"Every Sunday. It's the only way I can catch up on the indexing." She sat down at her desk. "I saw Marmelli on the elevator. Aristotle Onassis died last night. The weekend editor ordered him in to go through the AP and UPI."

"Beware the Ides of March."

"The way he complains, you'd think he never works weekends."

"He doesn't. Not often."

"He asked if I'd heard of T. Bone Walker."

"He's dead?" He turned in the chair to look at Mrs. Wiggins. "Yes."

"One of the greats."

"Don't I know it? Marmelli isn't even running a short. I saw T. Bone perform down in the Village." Mrs. Wiggins sounded wistful. "That was a thrill."

"When did you see him?"

"Don't sound so incredulous. Just after the war."

"I'm impressed. And surprised."

"Yes, I'm sure. Librarians lead long and interesting lives. You'll eventually learn that." She picked up a thick stack of clips from the desk. "Take these. After you left Friday, I found something in the legal notices that might be of interest."

"Legal notices?"

"Certainly." She said it like he should already know the why when he didn't even know the what. "An intriguing tale of salt. In November, Clean Streets, Inc., won the road salt contract advertised by the city. I went back to the year prior and found another firm, Garibaldi & Winkle, got that same contract. In fact, Garibaldi & Winkle had won it for twenty straight years."

"You have my attention."

"A five-and-a-half-million dollar contract. Over twenty years, it was worth close to sixty million dollars to Garibaldi. Who's the city lawyer that awards these?"

"Constable McNally."

"Quite right. That's why I started looking at the legal notices. These companies are what you would call 'dirty.'"

"How dirty?"

"Both connected to organized crime."

"How do you know that?"

"I read every newspaper published in the city. I file. I cross-index. I remember. They're mentioned here. They're mentioned there. That's why these particular notices jumped out at me. They're most certainly connected to the syndicates. Call your sources at the police department. Do a reporter's job on this. That's why you're here, isn't it?"

Taylor opened his mouth and shut it again.

"That's right. There is nothing you can say."

Taylor picked up the phone and dialed Chumley's. His best source on organized crime, Detective Mark Murphy, used the bar in Greenwich Village as a base. The guy also still talked to him.

"You working?"

"Enjoying the brunch."

"Chumley's has a brunch?"

"My kind. They pour it." The cop already sounded three sheets to the wind. "What are you doing in on a Sunday?"

"I'm trying to track down two companies that bid for a city contract last year. The loser was Garibaldi & Winkle. You know it?"

"Sure, a front run by Karl Poborski. A mob player going all the way back to prohibition."

"What's he into?"

"Kickbacks on contracts, extortion, racketeering. Interesting character. He's the oldest surviving member of a Polish family shoved aside by bigger and deadlier Italian organizations."

"How about Clean Streets?"

"They're another one. Linked to the Grado family. You see both companies involved in the same dirty business. Which means you're going to find something wrong with that contract. Bribes, kickbacks. The usual shit."

"Anyone targeting Garibaldi?"

"You kidding? The department's too busy with drugs and muggings. The FBI, I mean, it's their fucking job. They haven't done shit since Watergate and Hoover kicked it."

"Contact info?"

"Hold on, let me check my little black book of bad behavior." He was gone about a minute. "Poborski lives at 3238 Netherland Avenue in the Bronx. He gives a lot of money to Saint Gabriel's Church on Arlington Avenue up there. That's his one financial excess. The only one anyone's found, at least. I don't have anything on Clean Streets. I'll phone you back."

"I appreciate this. How's things?"

"Shitty. I got busted down to the drug squad four months ago. Everyone's either high, corrupt, or scared shitless. And those are the cops. The city's a cesspool and I'm sliding into it."

He read more of the clips on Declan's grandfather, Big Johnny Scudetto. He took some notes, even though nothing really grabbed him. The mob connection to city contracts preoccupied his mind. Sunday afternoon was a great time to catch people at home. He decided to head up to the Bronx to talk to Poborski. His other leads were dead-ends. Besides, this was a good interview to do before meeting McNally in the morning.

He snuck out the same loading dock he'd used to enter the building to avoid Fedora and his boys if they were camped out in front of the *MT*. He rode the Broadway express, changed to the local and dozed for much of the ride. The nap turned down the volume on his hangover. He walked up to Netherland Avenue from Broadway. He still limped on his sore right ankle, which he'd taped before leaving the trailer. He'd come close to yelling when he put his shoe on and now had it tied as loosely as possible. At least he hadn't injured the left leg, which was where he wore his ankle holster. His head cleared as he approached Poborski's. A new lead always had that effect.

Poborski lived in a classic Riverdale Tudor. The homes in this Bronx neighborhood had yards, trees, hedges, and driveways. They were a socio-economic universe away from the South Bronx, a mere four miles south of here, where blocks were being torched weekly.

Taylor pressed the doorbell, setting off a multi-tone chime like a church bell. He put a piece of Teaberry gum in his mouth. The black wood door swung in, and a tall, heavyset man with thick white hair looked down on Taylor through the glass. His bulk was a mix of muscle and fat, giving him a curdled look, like an old bear—diminished but still dangerous. He held a dinner napkin in one hand.

"Mr. Poborski?"

"Who are you?" He wiped the corners of his mouth and checked around and behind Taylor. The habit of a wary man.

"Taylor with the *Messenger-Telegram*. I'm working on a story about Declan McNally—"

"Constable McNally's son? Such terrible news. Awful news. But we're in the middle of Sunday dinner right now."

"I only have a few questions. As you said, a terrible tragedy."

"I don't know what I can tell you."

"It will only take a little of your time."

Poborski pushed open the storm door. As Taylor stepped in, he met a wall of heat. Steam hissed from radiators. The house was a sauna. On top of the heat and humidity, almost mingled with it, the smell of boiled cabbage hung in the air. Poborski turned into the living room. The odor intensified and became oppressive. He pointed Taylor to a couch and sat in a chair next to it. The furniture was draped with gold slipcovers. On a low marble coffee table sat a crystal ashtray, a sterling silver cigarette holder, and a standing lighter big enough to weld steel.

Poborski indicated the cigarette holder. "Would you like a smoke, Mr. Taylor?"

"No thanks."

From the back of the house a commanding voice pitched high yelled something in Polish.

Poborski answered back at the same volume. "My wife, she does not like Sunday dinner interrupted." He smiled. "How can I help you? It's very terrible. A good family. A very good family."

"Do you know Constable McNally well?"

"I do business with the city. Lots of contracts. Of course I know him. I work with him very well. We feel very bad for him. Such a tragedy. We saw the whole family at the funeral mass."

"I've been doing some research on Mr. McNally's work. Your company won a road salt contract for two decades. Until last fall. Clean Streets got it."

"Sometimes you get outbid."

"Losing a deal like that must be major. Five and a half million dollars. Sixty million over twenty years. Serious money."

"So?"

"Violence is done for a lot less."

"What are you talking about violence? I'm a businessman. Contracts are won and lost every day. You're here harassing me on my Sunday. Yet the cops haven't bothered to talk to me. Even they're not so stupid."

"They have their methods. I have mine. Sometimes they don't show up until *after* they read about somebody in the paper."

"Is that a threat?" The smile was gone, replaced by a look of malignance.

More yelling from the direction of the kitchen.

Poborski snapped back a quick answer without looking away. The clock on a side table ticked. "Some people think I am tough. They have not met Mrs. Poborski. She believes in the old Polish customs. Sunday dinner is not interrupted."

Taylor knew the customs Poborski favored. He wasn't brave in any stupid way, but he knew he had one shot at this. Either that or cross Poborski off the list of leads worth pursuing. He wasn't a detective. He couldn't demand that the man come in for more questioning.

"My police sources tell me Clean Streets is a front for a syndicate run by the Grado family." An old gambit. Make Poborski's competitor sound like the bad guy in the story and maybe get a rise.

The old man gave an exaggerated I-don't-know shrug. "You will excuse me. I am a private American citizen. I do not need to be put through this." He stood up.

"Do you know Mark Voichek?"

"I have never heard of him." Exasperation tinged his voice now.

A muscular younger man, baldheaded with a goatee, appeared in the doorway. He folded his arms, and everything under his polyester shirt moved like live animals in a shiny green bag.

"My son, Sash, comes to bring me back to dinner. He is a good boy. He does everything Mrs. Poborski asks."

Taylor stood to leave. "This is what I know. Voichek is a homeless man." He remembered Voichek's rebuke. "Check that. A hobo. Three men attacked him and stole his clothes. That same night those clothes ended up on Declan McNally. The boy was left out on the street. Drugged into unconsciousness and soaked to the skin so he'd freeze to death."

"This is a very messy business you describe," Karl Poborski growled. "Sounds like it will get even messier. It's none of my business. I must eat my dinner. Good day to you."

Poborski departed down the hall. The younger man opened the front door with a look like he wanted to slam it into Taylor's head.

Taylor walked back to the subway station. Trying to get anything out of Poborski had been risky. Taylor knew that. But he'd learned a couple of things talking to that dangerous man. The police hadn't yet made a connection to the mobster. That could be good, if Taylor was ahead on the story. It could be bad, if he was barking up the wrong tree and that tree had an old bear in it. Taylor didn't think so. Poborski had wanted to end the conversation as soon as the salt contract came up, and not just because his wife was screaming at him. His demeanor had switched instantly from concern about the McNally family to anger.

The hangover was back full strength by the time Taylor boarded the subway. The hothouse cabbage smell had overwhelmed the nap and aspirin.

23

———◆———

TAYLOR STOPPED THREE blocks from Laura's apartment building and called into the *MT*.

"Two messages. Mr. Harry Jansen said to tell you 'nothing yet on Voichek.' Mr. Worth also left a message. He said, well let me see." The operator stopped.

"Yes?"

"It's a long one. 'Taylor, I know you're picking up messages here. So you must not be sick. Personnel says I don't have to wait until you come back. I'll have you out on your ass by five tomorrow. Be here after the page one meeting.' " She paused again. "I'm sorry. That was his language."

"It's not a problem."

"That man is always so rude when he calls in."

"He's rude to everyone."

A bastard. That's what Worthless really was. He circled two blocks at random and walked back down Lex, all to make sure no one was following him. He could save his job if he figured a way to keep Clare Kazka and her mom safe. There was the rub. Whatever he had by five tomorrow would be enough. Or it wouldn't. He'd deal with what came after … after. There wasn't time for worry.

He pushed Laura's buzzer. The speaker gave a muffled squawk. *Please don't let it be the roommate.* He couldn't bear spending the afternoon by himself.

"It's Taylor."

More squawking, the door buzzed, and he started up the stairs, going slowly to favor his hurt ankle. On the second landing, Laura met him with a hug. He balanced on his good leg and loneliness left like a chill chased away by a warm fire.

"Are you all right?"

"No worse for wear. I can walk, after a fashion."

"Why didn't you call and say you were coming? I only went out once to get the papers. I made Sarah Jane and Annie clear the hell out."

"I know it doesn't make any sense. I was afraid I'd find out you weren't here if I called. I didn't want to jinx it."

"Superstition instead of facts?" She smiled. "Of course I'm here. Come on up."

Taylor climbed slowly and this made her fuss over him even more. He liked it. He couldn't remember the last time anyone had. He eased onto the futon and asked for a glass of water and two Tylenol. Alternating with aspirin every two hours got more painkillers to his head and ankle.

"When are your roommates coming back?"

"Not for a while. Why?"

"I need a nap. I could drop off right here."

She looked disappointed, opened her mouth to speak but seemed to change her mind. "You sleep. I can read the Sunday papers. I went down to the newsstand and got the *Boston Globe* and the *Washington Post* too."

"That's a treat." He stretched, closed his eyes, and in moments, fell into blackness with a violent shudder. He opened them with another shudder convinced he'd dozed for only a few minutes. Laura sat under a cone of yellow light from a floor lamp, her face relaxed and beautiful as she read. The window behind framed buildings and a dark sky. Hours must have gone by during one of those deep naps that seemed to pass in a heartbeat.

"What time is it?"

"Quarter after seven."

He blinked his eyes and fought the desire to drop back down into wonderful sleep. "Thanks for letting me nap. Yesterday was one hell of a day."

"Tell me what's happened. I'm dying to hear."

He sat up and stretched his long legs in front of him. She moved onto the futon.

"Voichek split on me. He's panicked. I'm really worried about him."

He described the arrival of the mobsters the night before and his visit to Poborski. As he talked, she gently rubbed his neck.

"Your muscles are like iron cords."

"Please don't stop." He rotated his head as she massaged. "I have to find Voichek before they do."

"I'm sure he'll be okay."

"He doesn't know what he's up against, and I'm up shit creek. If Voichek doesn't turn up, I've got nothing. I like the guy. You need to meet him. There's a story there for you." He leaned back against her. "He's a walking dictionary for this old-time hobo language. You don't hear these words anymore. It'll make a great feature for the paper."

"You know I love anything about language." He again remembered making fun of her linguistics classes. He looked back but didn't see anything in her face that said she did. She added, "What about the mafia angle?"

"I didn't get anything solid from Poborski. Maybe there's something. I have to find a way to jimmy that door open. If the contract is tainted, McNally is corrupt. I've got these pieces, but I'm not sure if they're part of the same puzzle. McNally better give me some answers tomorrow. Worthless can do whatever the fuck he likes."

"What do you mean?"

"He's going to fire me at five."

"Asshole."

"It's been coming. I'm not sweating it. I was set up and the paper bought it. Now I know I'm in the clear. I'm on to a good story. I'm shoving this story down Worth's throat. Just hope I can get it in time."

She pulled him close and kissed him softly. "You lie back and relax. No napping, though."

"How could I?" He laughed and kissed her once before falling back onto the futon.

She gently kissed him as he slid one hand up her peasant dress. His hand rose on a smooth, firm thigh.

"Nothing like a Sunday afternoon."

"Nothing at all."

The kissing grew more passionate. Laura undid his belt and jeans. Their breathing came faster. She hiked up her dress and lowered herself onto him, started slowly, picked up speed, arched her back.

When they had both finished, she lowered her head to his chest. Her breathing was quick. "You like a little afternoon delight?"

"Oh yeah."

Sometime after, when he was half asleep, half awake, relaxed and happy, a siren, now two, came down Third Avenue. Laura raised her head to look out the window over his head. "Engine Three-Three and Truck Nine. The romantic symphony of New York."

She got up and made herself a cup of something called Lapsang Souchong tea. Taylor didn't get tea, and she already knew better than to force anything new on him. He didn't do well with new things. She brought him a milky Nescafé loaded with sugar. A small gesture, but a perfectly wonderful one. She was so easy to hang out with.

"Sunday evening's a balanced thing." Laura sipped and steam from the mug curled over her cheekbones. "It's too close to Monday to start big projects. There's really only enough weekend left to do nothing."

With that, she settled into one corner of the couch with the Book Review from the *Sunday Times*. Taylor picked up the *Daily News* to read the stories filed by the tabloid's top-notch police reporters. He found a pretty good one—hell, an excellent one—on a mob hit out on Staten Island, a netherworld populated by bad guys and cops indistinguishable from one another. Same houses, yards, schools, cars, and sometimes, even jobs.

He contemplated the Sunday evening doing nothing that Laura suggested. It sounded perfect, but perfect wasn't possible for him tonight. He rose from the couch.

"Where are you going?"

"I feel like I should be looking for Voichek. But to be honest, I don't know where to start. Won't until Harry Jansen comes up with something. Tomorrow I'll see Constable McNally." He rubbed his eyes. "There is one thing I've been avoiding. I have to tell the homicide detectives about Voichek. It can't be my secret anymore. Who knows? Maybe something crazy will happen and the cops will actually find him before the villains do. Either way, I can't sit on it any longer."

"I'll come with you. Be better than being with my roommates."

"The cops are going to yell at me."

"My roommates will do the same. Unless they yell at each other."

24

———◆———

THE DESK SERGEANT at the 10th didn't ask a single question when Taylor said he had information, instead sent them straight upstairs. The McNally case was four-star high priority.

NYPD Inspector Anthony Dellossi, in a crisply pressed shirt and wearing the gold eagle of his rank, knew Taylor. "Goddammit, if you bullshitted my sergeant to get up here to poke around—"

"Relax, Inspector. I've got something for you."

"What, you're checking it out before publishing?" He laughed darkly and returned to the file he was reading. "New one for you, Taylor."

"I interviewed a man named Mark Voichek. His clothes were on Declan McNally."

Dellossi looked up from the file. The small shiny brown eyes in his narrow face were easy to read. He thought he was smarter than you. He knew you were guilty.

"The field jacket with the flags and the patched jeans. They were stolen from Voichek by three hoods. They were going to kill him too, but he got away. They're still trying to kill him."

"Where is Voichek now?"

"I talked to him yesterday. He split last night. He's worried about getting killed."

"You let him?"

"What was I supposed to do? Make a citizen's arrest?"

"No, just place a fucking citizen's phone call."

"I spent most of yesterday running from the killers with him."

"All the more reason to come to us. I promise you, if we don't find him, I'll have you for something. Accessory after the fact. Obstruction. Trespass. Whatever. Anything. You can't fuck with an investigation."

"Fuck with it? I found the guy."

"What do you know about him?"

"He's a hobo. He lives on his wits and odd jobs."

"So, what you're telling me is this vagrant claims his clothes were stolen and put on Declan McNally. How do you know he's not the killer?"

"You wonder why the guy didn't want to come in?" Laura didn't stint on the sarcasm.

"Listen Miss—"'

"It's Laura Wheeler. Ms. Laura Wheeler."

"Taylor's in trouble here. You want to join him?"

"Easy, easy." Taylor held up his notebook. "Let's stay cool. I'll tell you what else I've got."

He provided a description of Voichek and the three hoods. He didn't give everything he knew about the McNally case, just everything about Voichek. Cops had burned him before. They'd buy a favor by giving one of his leads to another reporter. Or do it just to fuck with him.

"I better be able to corroborate the incident at the coffee shop." Dellossi stubbed his finger on his legal pad as if trying to pin Taylor's facts to the paper.

"You will. What have you got on the case?"

"I'll tell you when I tell the other reporters. Which will

be when we make an arrest. We are pursuing a number of promising leads."

"That's bullshit. I just gave you your only promising lead."

"Careful, Taylor." Dellossi smiled like he'd won a game they were playing. "You're lucky I don't sit you down with one of my stupider sergeants and have him interview you about all this for eight or ten of your Sunday night hours. We're done here."

Laura spoke as soon as they were out on 20th Street. "What a dick. That's how a senior officer acts?"

"They don't like it when you're out ahead of them."

"You must get that treatment a lot."

"Some. It's easy to take when that's what it means. I got something I wanted, though."

"What's that?"

"Confirmation. He didn't even hint at any leads, and that means he doesn't have anything. He'd want me to know if he's got something going. Too much ego. Too much political pressure. If we're out in front of the cops, we're out in front of the other papers." They walked to the corner. For the first time in a week, the temperature had climbed above the twenties. Positively balmy after the terrible March cold wave. "I'll check in with the switchboard. Then call it a night and get some rest. Five o'clock deadline tomorrow. Got to make something happen."

"I've been thinking about the Kazkas." She put her hand on his arm. "You really have to do something with that information."

"I can't put them in harm's way. Or spoil the trail to whoever set me up."

"There must be a way. You'd exonerate yourself at the *MT* in an instant."

He picked up the receiver, slid in a dime, and with it, mouthed a silent prayer for news of Voichek. There was news, but not the kind he wanted.

"Mr. Harry Jansen called forty minutes ago," said the

operator. "Here's his message. 'Torres the Kid saw Voichek on West Forty-fourth. Before he could catch up, three men chased Voichek. Torres followed. They headed onto the pier at Forty-third. Torres called from a pay phone across the street and said he was going onto the pier. I tried to stop him. Some of us are heading over. I hope numbers are enough. Please help if you can.'"

Taylor thanked the operator and hung up.

"I'm coming with you," Laura said.

"No. I don't know what's going on. It could be dangerous."

"It'll be dangerous for you too."

"This is all going in a bad direction. Please, go back and tell Dellossi about this and go to the paper and wait. Be my rewrite man."

"Man?"

"Man, woman. Whatever works." He waved down a cab.

"Take care, Taylor." Laura's voice trailed behind.

25

———◆———

THE BROKEN-DOWN THEATRICAL palaces on 42nd Street flashed past. One advertised "classic New York burlesque." The rest, triple bills of triple-X. ·

In light Sunday traffic, it took the cab ten minutes to reach the curb across the Westside Highway from the pier. That wasn't fast enough for Taylor. He was desperate to get there and keep a murder from happening. He was at least an hour behind the action. Taylor threw too much money at the cabbie, got out and ran across the street and along the front of the pier.

No police cars, marked or unmarked. No John Doe. No homeless. No sign of anyone. A garage-sized door into the covered pier stood ajar. Taylor easily squeezed through the gap. Dust circulated in the cold air of a long warehouse lit by security lights outside. Footprints on the floor showed a crowd had milled around and moved down the pier to the end. Taylor found the place where the big group stopped and a smaller party of three people separated and walked to a place where the boards were pushed apart. He leaned out of the hole. A body was splayed in the position of a drowned man forty feet below but kept from the water by the rock-hard ice of the Hudson.

Blood from Voichek's head stained the snow cherry red.

Bodies didn't bother Taylor. Yet the sight of this one forced him back inside. Defeat and despair grabbed hold of him. He hadn't kept the old man safe. The story was out of control, writing itself before he could. Killing people before he could stop it.

He guessed one thing from all the footprints in the dust. Jansen and his people must have already been there and left once they saw the body. Did Torres the Kid leave with them? Or had the thugs grabbed him? Another murder? If Torres followed Voichek and saw anything and escaped, he was now *the* link to the killers. If he was alive. "Ifs" were the enemy. Too many goddamn ifs. He should have kept Voichek with him. Or gotten him into police custody. His head spun. Things he hadn't done. Things he needed to do.

No other clues were evident, but he wasn't a Sherlock Holmes, not even an Anthony Dellossi. He needed to interview people to figure out what the hell was going on.

As he crossed the Westside Highway, a police car pulled up. He owed Voichek the time to see his body safe. A fire truck and ambulance followed, and two brave firemen crept out onto the ice. After a minute, they dropped a blanket over Voichek's body. The firemen loaded the body onto an aluminum stretcher and pulled the stretcher off the Hudson as if it were a sled in the Yukon.

Taylor turned away. He'd have time to mourn Voichek later. Nothing mattered but tracking down the murderers. A bus rumbled up 11th Avenue. He was happy to pay the fare to go six blocks to Jansen's improvised homeless shelter between 47th and 48th. The place was empty of people. The bundles, bags, and blankets were all gone. Only a stray item on the floor attested to a fast clear out. Taylor didn't blame them. Their people were being killed, and the *why* didn't matter. Safety did. Glowing embers faded in the fire pit, and darkness closed in around him. Nothing here would be any help.

A crash from behind.

He spun. Nothing. He thought of the revolver at his ankle, but that was a bad idea given the darkness and his poor aim. He picked up a two-by-four from a small stack of firewood and swung it in front of him, as much a blind man's cane as a weapon. He walked in the direction of the sound and found a doorway into a tented hallway.

"Hello?" Footsteps ran away. He pushed on, and the darkness became so complete it seemed to touch his eyes. He moved the club in a wider arc. The wood made a clunking noise as it hit the walls. "Who's there? I just want to talk."

A light flickered up ahead. Ten feet or a hundred? No way to tell. He wanted to close the distance but couldn't in the blackness. Bright light right in his eyes. Whiteout. A different kind of blindness. Running footsteps. Someone hit him hard and spun him, and he banged his forehead on a wooden support.

Taylor touched his head. No blood. He turned around once to get his bearings. Nothing. Around again and his eyes, recovering from the flash, found the doorway back to the main room, which in that blackness glowed as a rectangle of light from the dying fire's last bit of brightness. The runner passed through the doorway like a shadow. Taylor hustled to the door and got into the main room as the figure raced past the brick fire circle.

"Wait. I'm not going to hurt you."

That just spurred the figure on. The runner was faster than Taylor could manage with two good ankles. He or she was going to get out into the streets and disappear into Hell's Kitchen. Something on the floor gave Taylor an assist and tripped the runner. A flashlight spun across the floor. Taylor got there before the runner could get up.

"No! Please don't kill me."

"I'm not going to hurt you." Taylor held up the two-by-four like a club. He tossed it aside, and the clattering caused the boy to throw his hands over his head. Taylor gripped one arm and studied the small thing he'd caught.

"I didn't see nothin'."

"Torres the Kid?" The boy didn't respond. "I'm Taylor. Harry Jansen knows me."

"I've heard of Taylor, but how do I know you're him?" He tried to squirm out of Taylor's grip.

"I'm not attacking you, am I?"

He quit struggling, and Taylor let go so he could stand. A big purple knit ski cap was pulled down over the boy's ears. Dark hair curled from underneath it. A camel hair coat hung down to the tops of old-fashioned Converse basketball shoes.

"You're the one who writes about the dead. Is that why you're here? To get Voichek's death story?"

"No. I was hoping …. I wanted to find him alive. Did you see what happened?"

The coat was clean, as was his face. Torres the Kid took care of himself. Voichek was the one who taught him how to do that. Taylor let the wave of sadness rise, crash and retreat. No time right now to hold onto it.

"It was awful." Torres blew out an exhausted sigh. "I couldn't do anything. Anything. I hadn't seen Voichek for almost a week. Since Port Authority, right after he started hiding. I went to check one of his spots here on the West Side. A garage nobody uses. Just as I got there, he bolted with those hoods chasing. It was like a posse in the movies, where they go after the wrong guy. He *was* the wrong guy, right?"

"He was the wrong guy."

"Voichek ran onto the pier. That scared the hell out of me. Voichek taught me to never ever go down a dead end. I don't know why he did. Maybe he was already hurt. I peeked in. There's nowhere to hide, so I snuck up along the side flat against the wall. Voichek was facing me, and their backs were to me—"

"How many?"

"Three. One in an old man's hat and two in ski caps. Voichek saw me. I know because he shook his head a little and looked back at the door to say I should get out of there. Without warning, he charged one of the men wearing a ski cap. The tall hood in the hat laughed and watched for a couple of punches and went over and kicked Voichek. He kicked him and kicked him and kicked him until the only time Voichek moved was when that boot hit his body. Christ it was horrible. They threw him right off the pier. I started running. I've never been shot, but I was scared. I was sure I was going to find out what that feels like trying to get off the pier. No shots though. I hid across the street before they got outside."

"Did the men say anything?"

"While he was kicking Voichek, the hat, he spoke. 'You should have let us do you a week ago when no one cared. Worthless fucking bum. Worthless fucking bum.' I don't think Voichek could hear anything by then. I watched after they left. I was afraid they'd come back. Jansen and everyone showed up, went in and left again pretty quickly."

"Why didn't you go with them?"

"In case those yeggs were around. I was scared they'd follow my friends. I was scared they'd get me."

"You were smart."

"I wish." He looked down at his sneakers. "Voichek helped people. He always helped me. Why would they kill him?" His eyes welled up, but he wiped them with the baggy camelhair sleeve and stood stoically.

"Is Torres your last name?"

"I'm just Torres the Kid. I left the other names behind. Are you gonna turn me over to the bulls?"

Taylor had to smile a little at Voichek's hobo lingo. Maybe here was a way it would survive.

"I should, for your own protection."

A look of terror came over Torres. "You said—"

"Don't worry. I'll figure something out. Where do you think Jansen went?"

"Don't know. Everything is such a mess. People will use churches, Sally Ann, wherever they feel safe. We won't be back here soon."

Voichek murdered and Jansen's community destroyed. Taylor hadn't done much to help any of them. He had to make sure this kid was safe and then find the men who killed Declan McNally and Mark Voichek. He couldn't make things right. He could never make things right. He had a lifetime to feel bad. Right now, he'd do whatever he needed to do to stop the killing.

"Could you identify the three of them?"

"I dunno. Maybe. They were kinda far away. I'm not talking to any cops."

"Let's get you somewhere safe." That meant out of Hell's Kitchen.

They left the shelter and walked east on 48th toward Times Square. A block later, a shadow detached from the deeper shadow of the building in front of them and blocked their way. Torres the Kid reacted in an instant, racing back the other way toward 10th.

"Kid, wait!"

A second figure appeared—seemed to materialize on the sidewalk—and snatched the sprinting boy. The Kid gave one yelp and went quiet. Taylor pulled out the .32, closed the distance and leveled the gun.

"Let him go now."

One blow knocked the gun out of Taylor's hand. A leg swept and sent him crashing to the sidewalk. A fist with "KILL" tattooed across the knuckles grabbed a big clump of Taylor's field jacket and the other fist—this one read "OR BE"—pulled back to strike.

"No, not him." Torres the Kid grabbed the big fist. "He's the Writer for the Dead. He was looking for Voichek."

The bulky man pulled Taylor up to his feet and straightened his jacket.

"Sorry about that, man." The voice was an iron rasp. "Jansen had us watching the area. He thought Torres the Kid would come back. We didn't know what to expect. I'm McAfferty. This is Doonz."

McAfferty had a block head, flat line for a mouth and intelligent green eyes. The other man came up behind and made no impression in the dark except for his size. There was a lot of him.

"We'll take Torres." It wasn't a suggestion.

Taylor looked down at the boy. "You okay with that?"

"Sure I am. Jansen sent them, didn't he?"

"You can keep him safe?"

"I'm 101st Airborne. Doonz was Force Recon in 'Nam. We can take care of ourselves, and the rest. We're going to get him out of harm's way. After that, we find the fuckers who did in Voichek. That man was a decorated vet. We don't let that happen to a brother in arms. Bastards can't be allowed to think we're all crazies who will roll over or run away when they kill one of our own."

"You know the kid is a witness. He can ID the killers. The police will want to talk to him."

"They can when Jansen decides so."

"That's probably for the best." Taylor was dead on his feet and relieved the boy's people could protect him. Torres the Kid leaned against McAfferty. "Have Jansen contact me if you track the hoods down."

"You'll hear about it." There was a wickedness in McAfferty's voice.

The three walked toward 10th. Taylor turned and made his way to the muted glow of Times Square and the Howard Johnson. He sat down in the phone booth, closed the door, flipped through his notebook and outlined the story in his head. It was time to put what he had into print. He didn't give a rat's ass if that forced the killers out into the open. He hoped it did. He dialed the *MT* and asked for Laura.

"I've got a story on Voichek's murder. I'll dictate it to you. Get the night editor to take it as yours. How long have I got?"

"Forty minutes for the late city final."

"All right, here we go." He looked down at the notebook. "Dateline, Manhattan. The man whose clothes were used in the murder of city teenager Declan McNally was himself killed yesterday by three men who may be connected to the McNally homicide. Mark Voichek, a self-styled hobo of no known address, was beaten to death by the three men and pushed from the 43rd Street pier onto the frozen Hudson River, according to a witness. New graph. In an interview Saturday, Voichek said his clothes, including a World War II Army field jacket with more than 40 country flags sewn on both sleeves, were stolen by three men last Monday. McNally, the grandson of Manhattan Democratic Chief John Scudetto, was found dead in the same clothing the next morning in the Gansevoort Market. New graph."

Taylor fed ten paragraphs to Laura, who typed it out on her Selectric just as fast. She read the copy back to Taylor. "It's a good story."

"Thanks. There'll be a better one when I find out who these guys are."

He left HoJo's for the 42nd Street subway station, dozed off and on during the hour-long ride to Forest Hills. He stopped in at Ahab's to see if he had any messages. Danny said no. The beers on the bar looked good. Really good. They would make his tired, hung-over, blasted empty feeling go away. For a little while, at least. He stood by the barstool where Voichek drank his third rail. Probably his last one. With a heavy heart and a deep longing for a beer, and for Laura, he left Ahab's and crept up the alley across the street from his burnt-out house. Tired as he was, he checked the blocks on either side for a stakeout before approaching. He pushed open the trailer door—the lock was still busted—with the small revolver in the lead. The Airstream was cold and dark. And empty. He shoved the cooler up against the door. That didn't make him feel much more secure. He stripped off his pants, eased his legs up on the narrow bed, and lay back, the Smith & Wesson in his hand on his chest. He couldn't get rid of the image of Voichek's body on the river, his blood staining the ice the color of a cherry snow cone.

PART VII:
Monday, March 17,
1975

26

———◆———

Taylor rode the E train to the World Trade Center and took the stairs up to Church Street. New York's twin tallest buildings climbed in front of him. They'd been half-empty since construction finished in '73 right as the oil shock deepened the recession. The Port Authority only managed to convince a few government agencies to lease space in the massive white elephants, now offering the best view in New York. He'd never been up to the top. He didn't come here much. Downtown wasn't police-beat territory. Sure, money got stolen. It just wasn't considered a crime.

He'd woken an hour earlier with the image of Voichek dead still in his head and couldn't get it out. Fury rose in him as cold as the ice the old man died on. A collage of faces. His brother Billy, Declan McNally in the morgue, Harry Jansen, Voichek alive, Torres the Kid, Claire Kazka, Voichek dead. South Vietnam was falling. New York was failing. The only thing he could do in all the misery was track down the murderers before someone else got killed. The next step was to interview Declan's father. Mob involvement in city contracts intrigued Taylor. Constable McNally was in charge of the city contracting, and mobsters were tied up with two bidders last fall. Families had been targeted by the mob before. He liked the lead a lot. That, and he still didn't know enough about Constable's relationship with his son.

He crossed Murray Street in front of City Hall, a building dwarfed by the city it governed. It was scaled to fit in the square of a town upstate rather than a world capital. Behind City Hall climbed the Municipal Building, forty stories of towers, columns, and arches that looked like the skyscraper version of a wedding cake. More than a dozen city agencies filled it with the vast sprawling bureaucracy that was supposed to keep the city going. In this monster, City Hall's best-laid plans often went straight off a cliff.

He found the right elevator—thirty-three of them rose up into the Municipal Building—and rode to the 12th floor. The reception area was empty, including the desk guarding the way. The sign on the wall read:

CITY OF NEW YORK
DEPT. OF LAW

Taylor walked past several offices each stripped down to a desk and a chair. Even the lawyers got chopped as the city fell into a financial sinkhole. He found law department staffers at their desks; they pointed in the direction of Constable McNally's office but refused to say anything more. All attorneys dealt with journalists the same way. They told you nothing unless it served their purpose, and then you couldn't shut them up.

Outside McNally's office sat a secretary typing on a gray electric Smith Corona. The machine clattered like something from the steam age. The woman wore a dowdy blue suit and a frilly white blouse an old lady would choose. She was young, though, and probably shapely underneath all that cloth.

She caught him staring. "Can I help you?"

"Taylor from the *Messenger-Telegram*. Mr. McNally is expecting me."

"I'll buzz."

McNally met him at the door. His hair looked like it hadn't seen a comb since the funeral two days before. "Thanks for stopping by."

"How are you doing?"

"Not good, I'm afraid. Not even as well as can be expected." He shook his head slowly. "My life is filled with empty phrases like that. Come in."

The office was filled with flower arrangements that gave off a funeral-home odor of death. Probably all sent by contractors who worked with the city. Why else deliver them to the office? The flowers' scents mixed oddly with cigarette smoke, which hung in a cloud at the ceiling. Taylor took one of two unmatched guest chairs.

McNally pulled out a Chesterfield, lit it, took a long puff, and held it to the side. "I read the story on the killing of the homeless man. Written by Laura Wheeler. I thought you were working on this?"

"She is too."

"What else do you know?"

"That's most of it. Your son was wearing the clothes stolen from Mark Voichek. Voichek was murdered yesterday. I have very basic descriptions of the three hoods."

"Good lord." McNally took a long drag like he was inhaling for a deep dive. "How did his clothes get on Declan?"

"Last Monday night Voichek was jumped in an alley off West 46th by the same three. They wanted a homeless man. He bolted because he was convinced they were going to kill him. He was right. My guess now, but it's still a guess: the three men drugged Declan with barbiturates, soaked him down, dressed him in the clothes, and left him so the cold would finish the job."

"Still, Voichek could've been involved. Maybe that's why they killed him."

"I don't believe that. I talked to him. We were both chased on Saturday by these men. The people I know in the homeless community vouch for him. He was disposable. An innocent man pulled into a plot to disguise your son's murder as the death of a street person."

"You're doing a fucking better job than the detectives."

"I still need to ID the three men. What I really need is a motive for Declan's killing. I've got nothing. Is it possible there's some connection to your work?"

"My work?" McNally knocked his cigarette's long ash off in a steel ashtray with a miniature Statue of Liberty in the middle.

"You award city contracts worth millions. Money is murder's second favorite motive."

"This job ...." He waved over the desk piled with papers like it would explain what he was talking about. "What I am is a jumped-up purchasing manager. That's it. I buy staples and carpeting and tires for the city. That's nothing anyone is going to kill over."

"I've been looking into some of those contracts. There was one last November. Garibaldi & Winkle lost the road salt bid. They'd had the contract for twenty years. It went to Clean Streets, Inc., instead. What happened there?"

"Who knows? I'd have to check the files. Clean Streets must have been the low bidder. That's how it works around here. I'm a guy buying crap for the lowest possible price."

"It's that simple?"

"Pretty much."

"What if there were mob ties?"

"What do you mean?"

"Garibaldi is run by a mobster named Karl Poborski. Clean Streets is connected to the Grado family."

"That's easy. The Feds are supposed to let me know if a company is connected to organized crime. They don't win bids.

If Clean Streets got it, they must have been, well, clean, at that time certainly. I really should check all this. I handle hundreds and hundreds of contracts a year. Everything is a blur. Except Declan." He tapped his graying temple. "He's clear as day. And he's the one who's gone."

"Bribes and extortion have been a part of contracting for as long as there's been a City of New York."

"Are you suggesting I'm corrupt?"

"I'm not suggesting anything. Bad guys get city contracts and bad guys kill people. If you say you aren't involved in that sort of thing, great. I haven't found a motive for someone in Declan's life to kill him." He was stretching it there. Drug dealing got you killed. Laura was up at Columbia checking out that lead. McNally didn't need to know that yet. "Please go through your files. Think hard about it. Is it possible someone killed Declan to get at you?"

"If he's dead because of me …. Well, I don't know what I'd do." The phone rang. McNally looked surprised, as if it had never happened before. "Yes, I'll be right down." He stood and smiled weakly. "I'm sorry. That was the boss. Apparently there's a reporter roaming the halls. He wants to ask me about it. He doesn't like reporters. You should probably leave."

"You'll check those files?"

"Yes, yes. Garibaldi & Winkle. Sorry, the other one?"

"Clean Streets."

"Right." He moved a stack of files and wrote on a yellow legal pad underneath. "So much paper around this goddamned place. Meaningless paper."

McNally walked to the end of the hall and turned left. The secretary's chair was empty. Taylor took the elevator down and crossed the cavernous lobby. The worker ants of city government jostled him. A tap on his elbow.

"Mr. Taylor?" McNally's secretary already looked better just getting out from behind the desk. There was more than the hint of a figure under her frumpy clothes. "I'm Wendy Marlow.

Is Mr. McNally going to be all right? I'm so very worried about him."

"Call me Taylor. I don't know. It's awful what he's dealing with."

"It's hit him so hard." She looked to either side. Did she want to say something else?

"Would you have time to talk? You know, explain how things work up there? It might help him."

"My lunch hour is at noon. Meet me at the Gaiety Delicatessen on Worth."

"Great, I'll buy."

She seemed to like that.

He left the Municipal Building and headed west on Worth until he came to the deli. The scent of glorious hot pastrami and yeasty doughy bagels filled the air. He was now a traitor to Grandpop and the Greek clan of the coffee shop. Coffee shop people never ever went to delis. They were the *enemy*, according to Grandpop. Greeks could open as many diners as they liked, around corners from each other if they saw fit. That was fine. They were all fighting the same fight against the delis for the allegiance of New Yorkers.

He checked his watch. He had about an hour to kill, so he ordered a cup of coffee and sat down at the pay phone. He picked up one irate message from Inspector Dellossi and called the cop right away.

"Goddammit, Taylor. If you don't help me, I won't help you."

"I told you Voichek was in trouble. That was me helping you. You were more concerned with confirming my story than pursuing the investigation. Now Voichek's dead."

"That's right. Dead. All for a goddamn story. The NYPD could have protected him."

"But would you have? He didn't think police custody was safe."

"Deal with the guilt any way you like. Laura Wheeler said

you interviewed someone who witnessed Voichek's murder. I need to talk to that witness."

"She put everything the witness told me in her story."

"That's not fucking good enough. You're not a cop. God only knows what you missed. I need the witness in here."

"This is a scared teenager. Homeless too. I don't know where he is."

"I'm tired of this shit. You're writing stories, not running an actual investigation."

"Here's one of my actual angles. I'm looking at Constable McNally. He's in charge of city contracts. Can be a very dirty business. A mob outfit, Garibaldi & Winkle, lost a five-and-a-half-million-dollar contract last fall. It's run by Karl Poborski."

"McNally told us he's received no threats. None related to his work. None related to anything."

"Did you dig deeper?"

"I've no good reason to turn a murder case into a corruption investigation." Dellossi's overbearing confidence was getting on Taylor's nerves. "Certainly won't on one of your hunches."

"You don't want to investigate an ex-cop who's also the son-in-law of the Democratic boss."

"Not without good cause. The man has just lost his son. He's a grieving victim, not a suspect."

"What about Declan's drug dealing?"

"Some Eli students told us about it. That's off the record, of course."

Taylor wrote it down anyway. "Of course. What isn't with you? Is it true?"

"We haven't any proof yet."

"Drugs lead to murder."

"That's why I have a detail working the Columbia campus full-time. I'm not clear on what you're looking for. The sexiest angle for your next story? Mobsters? Drugs? Some of both? Must be hard to top a nine-year-old smack addict."

"'Facts *are* stubborn things.'"

"I'll pull you in if I have to."

"Let me know if you get anything on Poborski or the drug dealing."

"Don't hold your breath."

Taylor left the phone booth and ordered another coffee and a taste of the forbidden deli fruit, chopped chicken liver and Ritz crackers. He was going over his notes from McNally and Dellossi when Wendy Marlow sat down.

"It's so good to get out of there."

"You don't like working for McNally?"

"Oh no. He's wonderful. It's the rest of them. They all hate us."

"They?"

"The lawyers in our department."

"Why?"

"Because we're shaking things up, *of course.*" Marlow's husky voice took on a conspiratorial tone like Taylor was already in on the drama of her office life. She stopped to order chicken salad on white with a Dr. Brown's Black Cherry. Taylor asked for hot pastrami on rye with mustard and said he was done with the plate in front of him.

"Exactly how are you shaking things up?"

"Well, it's not me, actually." She laughed and her blue eyes shone. She could be really pretty. Had McNally seen that? "I just help Mr. McNally. He does things differently than the other guys. They don't like it. You know why?"

"I don't." He didn't want to. Or need to. The petty politics of the city's legal department were going to get him nowhere but closer to Worth's deadline with no story.

"It all means more work for them. They're lazy."

"Mr. McNally says this?"

"No, the other secretaries. When they still talked to me. Now I'm the enemy. Just like Mr. McNally is the enemy of their bosses." The smile stayed in place. She seemed to like being in the office war, fighting at her boss' side.

"Did the other lawyers ever threaten McNally?"

"Oh no. They're not brave. All they do is gossip. I think they're scared of him. He was a policeman, you know."

This was a dead end. All he wanted to do was get back to the *MT's* morgue. She talked more. He ate his sandwich, flipped pages of his notebook and read his notes on the city contracting again. Why not run it past the secretary?

"Do you remember the road salt contract that went out at the end of last year?"

"God, what a commotion. Of course I do. In November."

"What kind of commotion?"

"It was such a *huge* scene. People still talk about it. Mr. Poborski stormed into the office—"

"Karl Poborski of Garibaldi & Winkle?"

"Sure. The day the contract went to Clean Streets." She leaned in, and her eyes went wide. "He comes to our office and starts yelling at Mr. McNally. Really screaming. Mr. McNally closes the office door. I can still hear. God, the things he said. 'We take care of each other. You remember that. Your fucking father-in-law knows. I guess you're not really *family,* are you?' He storms out and slams the office door like he's in a Broadway play. Everybody up and down the hallway was looking."

"When McNally and I talked, he didn't remember the contract."

"Oh, well." She reddened and appeared flustered. She'd contradicted the boss. She reached for the Dr. Brown's and pursed fuchsia lips around the straw. "It must be his grief. He really isn't himself. I feel so bad for him."

"Maybe that's it. Odd, though." He circled her version of Poborski's quotes. Hearsay, but damning hearsay. "Poborski brought up Big Johnny. What is McNally's relationship with his father-in-law like?"

"They talk on the phone a lot. I don't really know anything about the family. We're totally professional in the office." She smoothed her skirt twice with palms flat. Marlow thought she'd helped her boss by meeting Taylor. Most people who sat down for interviews convinced themselves of the same thing right before burying their spouse-lover-friend-boss under a pile of indiscreet quotations. "Mr. McNally is a good man. He was good to me. He was going to help me prep for night school so I could get my law degree. I'm sure that's another reason the other girls despise me. They want to stay *girls*. Marry someone and move to Long Island. I hate them all."

"He *was* good to you. Something's changed?"

"Since all this. We used to talk all the time. About all kinds of things. He's my only friend in that office."

"Was he more than a friend?"

"No." She stiffened. "I told you. It was all very professional."

"If you know something about his personal life that might help, you should tell me."

"God, no! I understand he loves his wife. I'm always here for him. That's all."

Taylor wrote "relationship??" and paid for lunch. "I'm coming back with you. I need to ask him a couple more questions."

"Oh, he's gone by now."

"Gone?"

"A Democratic function. St. Patrick's Day, of course."

"Where?"

"He didn't say."

"I'll catch up with him then. Can I call you if I think of anything?"

"You can call me about anything, anytime." Wendy Marlow held her chin up as she left the deli. She wasn't smiling anymore. There was sadness in her defiance somehow.

Why had McNally lied about the contract? If everybody in the office remembered the argument, McNally must. The Poborski connection looked more and more a part of the story. On the other hand, why would Poborski wait five months to exact revenge for losing the deal? Why would McNally lie when the truth would make the mobster the top suspect?

Unanswered questions were always the sign of a good story. A good story took time. With a deadline of five and Voichek dead, time was the one thing he didn't have.

27

———◆———

TAYLOR CHANGED TRAINS from the local to the express and back again to confirm no one was tailing him. He'd published the first story to flush out the killers. That didn't mean he wanted to get jumped by thugs. He needed to stay alive to finish this. He'd check in with Laura, do one piece of writing he had to finish now, and then track down McNally. That man had answers he needed.

In the MT's morgue, he lugged Mrs. Wiggins' Selectric to the study carrel, rolled in a piece of copy paper and went over his notes on Voichek one last time. What had started him on this story? The dead boy, nameless, homeless, down in the morgue. He'd needed a story to escape obits. He'd needed to know he could do something about one lost boy even if he could do nothing about another, his brother Billy, abandoned in the jungle during the forever war that was finally ending. His pursuit of the story hadn't helped the homeless one goddamn bit. One had been murdered and many more attacked. Stories had consequences. Most reporters denied that in their pose as impartial observers. Taylor was learning. Stories changed the world. And not always for the better.

He started typing his last obituary.

> Mark Voichek, a hero of World War II, hobo since the Great Depression, and resident of this city for the past several years, "took the Westbound" on Sunday. He was killed by unknown assailants on the pier at 43rd Street and the Hudson River.
>
> Voichek, who lived on the streets here in the city, was known for wearing a U.S. Army field jacket with its sleeves covered in flags of the world, which he put there to honor the peace for which he'd fought. He won two Purple Hearts and a Bronze Star and fought for the U.S. Army in Africa and Italy, according to those who knew him.
>
> Voichek still spoke the hobo language, a vast collection of terms coined by the people who rode the rails and stayed in camps by the millions beginning in the Great Depression. In that lingo, he called himself a "bridger," which meant he bridged the era from steam trains to diesel. He worried his language, descriptive of trains, hobo camps and good food, would soon die out with the last of the hobos.

He read it over, made a couple of corrections, folded it and put it in his pocket. One way or the other, he'd written his last obit. It wouldn't run if he didn't keep his job. Everything tied together. The phone rang.

"Dickie Bennett called." Laura's voice was urgent. "He saw the Voichek story. He has something that will help. He says it's important."

"Dickie Bennett?" Working to place the name, he reached for his notebook.

"The yearbook photographer. You talked to him at Eli. When I tried last Friday, he got all hinky."

"Right. He pointed me to the lacrosse players. Acted liked

there was something else he knew."

"He's still being cryptic. I'm in a coffee shop on the Westside. He wants to meet here after school."

"Did he give a clue what it's about?"

"No. Hold on a sec." A low murmur. "He's here. I'll call after we talk."

Taylor was caught between the need to hope and worrying he wasn't doing enough. He couldn't help but think of things he should have suggested Laura ask Dickie Bennett about the drug dealing. "I'm a complete horse's ass," he said aloud. Suggestions would have been the worst thing. Did he trust Laura? Could he trust anyone enough to work with them? Was he ever going to change? He wasn't sure and now he had to keep it simple. Step one, nail his part of the story. He left the morgue to track down Constable McNally. These weren't questions for the phone. He rode the subway to Hunter College and headed east to First Avenue. By the time he reached for the doorknocker of the townhouse on East 69th, his fingers tingled from the Arctic air.

Lydia McNally wore an ankle-length black dress, something for mourning but still sleek and stylish. She looked at him for long seconds, working to make the connection, but held up her hand before he could explain.

"Oh, the reporter. Come in. The maid and cook are off. My husband insists on hiring only Irish. They're off today and every other goddamn holy day." She led the way down the hallway. The dress whispered as she moved.

They passed the living room and the darkened dining room with dinner set for one. She kept going, all the way to a room at the back of the house with an overstuffed couch, a wingback chair, and a large RCA television in a dark maple cabinet. Lydia McNally settled onto the couch, tucking her legs under her. Newspapers were spread everywhere. On the floor, on all the tables, on the couch next to her.

"Have a seat."

"I'm actually looking for your husband."

"Thank God I don't have to be at that party drinking green Budweiser. Happy fucking St. Patrick's Day." She lifted a glass in toast. "Please talk for a little bit."

Taylor stepped around pages from the *Post*, *Messenger-Telegram* and *Times*. Another stack sat on the wingback.

"Just put those on the coffee table."

He moved the pile and sat on the smooth, worn leather.

"You can get comfortable here. We all do. Or did. Declan made us call this the rumpus room. I used the word once when he was little and he laughed and laughed. 'I want to rumpus,' he said. He was such a sunny, funny little boy. It's amazing the thousands of stupid things you turn into memories. You don't realize how much pain you're setting yourself up for. They're all over this house."

"It must be very hard."

"We'd come here to watch TV, to talk. To sit and read. He did his homework here until Con made him move to his room. He thought Declan wasn't being rigorous enough with his schoolwork. Whatever the hell that means."

"Your husband argued with Declan about schoolwork Sunday night."

"Declan was on a tear. I don't blame Con for what happened." She said it a bit too emphatically, as if answering an accusation. "It's not his fault. What I really want to know is why they can't find the fuckers who murdered my son." She waved at the papers all over the rumpus room. "I go through these every day because I'm being told nothing by anyone. Nothing for a week. Nothing until your paper runs that story about the dead bum whose clothes were stolen. The cops have nothing. Con and my father tell me to be patient with nothing. I'm tired of fucking nothing." She got up and went to a portable bar made of brass and glass and mixed another screwdriver, three-quarters vodka, one-quarter OJ. "You want something?"

"No thank you."

"Suit yourself." She took a sip and looked at him with intense dark eyes. "You found Declan. What did he say at the end?"

"I found his *body* at Bellevue. I have no idea what he said."

"You talked to the ambulance drivers, didn't you? He must have spoken to them. Did he know we loved him? What were his last words? Did he forgive us?"

"Forgive you for what?"

"Letting that happen to him." She burst into tears, standing next to the bar, letting loose her grip on the glass so that it spilled watery orange on the newspapers with a sound like rain on a rooftop.

"I'm sorry. To my knowledge, Declan spoke to no one before he died."

"No one? No one! What the fuck good are you? What a goddamned mess. I'm his mother, and I can't get any answers." She slumped onto the couch. "Con is at Murphy's on Second Avenue. With all the other mick Democrats drinking to their saint."

The telephone rang. Lydia McNally looked at the newspapers next to her, anger replaced by fear. She pushed the papers out of the way and found the princess phone. "I told you—" She listened. "Stop, stop, stop. I told you. I give him your messages. Leave us alone."

She slammed the phone down.

"What's wrong?"

"He keeps calling. I give Con the messages. Con screams at me like I'm making the call up or something. Now he's making threats."

Lydia McNally had buried the lead. It was a habit of bad journalists, old people, and the panic-stricken.

"Who's making threats?"

"This Polock Poborski."

"What did he say?"

"It's always the same. 'Your husband and I had an arrangement. If he doesn't honor it, tell him I will take steps he would not like.' I'm scared. Why doesn't Con tell the police?

We've been married twenty-three years. I don't know what's going on with him now." She looked at the TV and paused for so long Taylor thought she'd forgotten he was there. "*Gunsmoke* will be on tonight. We loved watching that together. Marshall Dillon. There's a man who hunts down killers. No bullshitting around."

She blew her nose and drank a third of the screwdriver.

28

———◆———

TAYLOR STEPPED OFF the bus on Second Avenue and walked two blocks to Murphy's. All the bars and restaurants he passed, whether Irish or not, displayed green paper shamrocks in their windows. Green Budweiser at ten cents a glass was the night's big special. Wasted men and a few women weaved from bar to bar looking for the better celebration. Would he find McNally loaded? Sometimes that made interviewing easier. Or made it impossible.

His press pass won him immediate entrance to the Democrats' party. Men in off-the-rack, three-piece suits filled the pub. A good portion of them wore green paper leprechaun hats, some only the torn-off brims. Cigarette smoke swirled thick in the air, mingling with the odor of beer and cheap cologne. "Danny Boy" started on the jukebox, and loud off-key singing drowned out Bing Crosby's tenor. Someone put a glass in Taylor's hand. Easter-egg green swirled through the beer. He set it on the bar.

In a break between songs, he asked two men midway down the bar for Constable McNally. One slurred something and stumbled into Taylor, spilling his beer everywhere, including down Taylor's pants. The second pointed and told him to look in the back room with Big Johnny and the other "top knots." Before Taylor could thank him, the man started doing something between a jig and an off-center whirl. Past the spinning man, at the bar's front door, Fedora stood with his two knit-capped goons. They were trying to talk their way in.

How the hell had they tracked him down? He'd been so careful all day. He thought of Poborski's call to Lydia McNally. What if it wasn't him? Maybe they were after Constable McNally. Excitement and fear together. He wasn't just on the hunt for McNally. He was in the middle of it.

Taylor moved back through the crowd to a doorway guarded by a uniformed policeman. He went to go through, and the cop held up his arm. "Private part of the party, sir."

"I'm looking for Constable McNally."

"Don't know him."

"He's an ex-cop."

"Lot of those celebrating."

Up at the front, the three men were inside the pub and standing at the corner of the bar, looking around the place. Taylor could try to convince this cop the three men were murderers. That would get all four of them hauled off for a night and day of questioning. The detectives would demand he produce Torres the Kid before doing anything. Which he couldn't. No, he must play this out. Fast and careful all at the same time. A room guarded by a cop might keep the killers out. No matter what, he had to talk to McNally first.

"How about Big Johnny Scudetto?"

"Who are you that wants to see him?"

"Taylor with the *Messenger-Telegram*."

Even beat cops knew the party chief always talked to reporters. The policeman opened the door and disappeared into the gloom and quickly returned.

"Says he'll see the man from the *Empty*." He indicated Taylor should follow.

The private area was less crowded than the front of the bar, with room for most to sit at wooden tables. The cop stopped in front of the biggest. Directly opposite sat a man with a fat smiling face and a fatter belly. Big Johnny's large head was bald but for white frizz on the sides. Three other men at the table laughed too loudly at something Big Johnny just said.

"Thank you, Officer," said Big Johnny.

The policeman turned and left.

"Isn't it wonderful how our Polock friends help on this special day?"

"I didn't realize Scudetto was Irish. What county are your people from?"

"Funny man. You work on the comic strips?"

"No, cops."

"Not anymore. You're the one who got nailed for making up that kiddie addict."

Taylor's face grew hot. A professional had called him a liar. He should know better than to underestimate Big Johnny. You didn't get to run the Manhattan Democrats without knowing all the dirt on everyone.

A woman in a tight green polyester dress slipped into the seat next to Big Johnny. She leaned her firm curves into the soft side of his large stomach, kissed him on the cheek and giggled.

"I hope you believe in the glass-in-hand rule." Big Johnny picked up a glass.

"Excuse me?"

"With glass in hand, *everything* is off the record." The woman kissed him again. He returned it this time, though not as long as the woman wanted. "Easy, Celebration, easy. Taylor, this is my friend, Celebration Jones. The glass?" He poured a second and offered it.

Celebration looked at Taylor with the hungry eyes of a woman kept from what she wanted.

"Right, glass in hand." Taylor took the beer, toasted and

took a small sip. "I'm following up on the investigation of your grandson's murder. I was told your son-in-law is back here."

"You figured out the ME had my grandson's body in Bellevue and didn't know it." Glittering brown eyes too small for the big head looked at him over the glass. "You did well on that one at least."

"I'm not done yet."

"I'm rolling some fucking heads over it. Why do you need Constable?"

"I've got some questions about city contracts."

Big Johnny frowned. "Contracts? I don't understand."

"I'm looking into a road salt contract."

"In connection with the murder? You're not serious? No one would be stupid enough to kill my grandson over a city contract. There's some murdering lunatic out there. The cops know they'd better find the psycho and put him down. And fast. Constable is over in the corner with the other city attorneys and the boys from the DA's office. You'll know them. All frowns and furrowed brows."

Taylor left as Celebration Jones wriggled onto Big Johnny's lap. The three men watched Big Johnny and his mistress as if the two were putting on a show for them.

The door to the back room remained closed. Yet Taylor didn't really feel safe, not even in a room with New York's top Democrat and a police guard outside. His only hope was to close in on the story before it closed in on him.

Six men sat at two round tables pushed together. Pitchers, half-empty cups, and overflowing ashtrays littered the tabletops. All of the men had turned their chairs so they could watch what was going on in the rest of the private room. A speaker above the table blared a song about whisky.

Taylor leaned down and spoke loudly to the nearest man. "Mr. Scudetto said Constable McNally is over here."

"Was. You missed him, sport. Just left." The man was short, angry and drunk.

"Any idea where he went?"

"Not a fucking clue." He turned away and started arguing with another lawyer about whether to throw money in the hat for the Irish Republican Army.

On the other side of the table, Taylor recognized a man named Lowenstein, a slump-shouldered lawyer who no-commented him that morning at McNally's office. He pulled up the chair opposite.

"We met this morning. Taylor from—"

"I know who you are. You're with the *Empty*. You're sniffing around our *good* friend McNally."

It was a nudge-and-a-wink line that wouldn't have fooled another drunk.

"Actually, I'm investigating the murder of his son."

"Journalis' as crusader." Lowenstein slurred and knocked back a shot. "*Casey Crime Photographer.*"

"Haven't heard of him."

"A show on the radio when I was a kid. Only place reporters ever solve crimes is on radio and TV."

A gray-haired man on the right hiccupped. "*The Sha-ah-dow* was better."

"McNally left." Lowenstein pointed at the door.

"Do you know where he went? Mr. Scudetto said you guys could help me out."

"No idea. He's the last guy I want to talk about today. Any day for that matter. I don't care what the fat man says."

"How long ago did he leave?"

"Man, if it will get you to quit pooping our party ... the cop at the door came over a half hour ago and told him his wife was on the phone. McNally, he's the usual peach. Says he told the bitch to leave him alone this afternoon. Goes out. Comes back even angrier, grabs his coat and splits. I tried to tell him the party after is always better than this. He ignored me like he always does. Like he doesn't have to listen to anyone. Typical. He's an asshole."

Bad things were going to happen tonight because everyone was crocked on their ass. Didn't help that the cop lied to him about knowing whether McNally was there. No surprise. Cops hated answering questions more than they liked asking them. He'd lost precious time in the hunt. He needed to know what McNally learned from his wife. He peered out the door into the main bar. The three killers were nowhere to be seen. Maybe they learned McNally left, which would confirm they were after McNally and not Taylor.

He left the bar for a phone booth on the street and dialed the McNallys.

"Did your husband come home?"

"I don't know where the hell he went."

"What did you tell him?"

"Poborski called again. After you left. I told him he'd find Con at that damn bar. Con can settle with him. He was furious at me for telling Poborski. I'm so tired of all his bullshit. It's like he's afraid of the guy. He can't stand up for his family."

That information brought the thugs to Murphy's. Taylor leaned against the booth for a minute to think. Poborski had threatened McNally and sent the three men who killed Voichek. Poborski had to be behind the murders of Voichek and Declan McNally. Back around he came to the one thing he didn't get. Why hadn't McNally reported Poborski? The contracts. Must be. McNally took bribes and he couldn't finger Poborski or he'd end up revealing his crimes. If so, he'd paid an awful price. A dead son. The murder unsolved. The story led straight to Poborski in the Bronx. He had to prove the connection between Poborski and the three killers.

Before leaving, he made two more calls. Laura was still out. He longed to talk to her before heading to the Bronx. Had she learned anything from Dickie Bennett?

Jansen answered right away at his pay phone.

"Are the vets around who took Torres the Kid from me?"

"They can be. Why?"

"I'm going to see the man who ordered the murders."

"What do you want them to do?"

"I need witnesses. Help, if things get out of hand. I know your guys are extremely capable. That's why I called. I want eyes and ears but not vigilantes. Last night they made it sound like they might take things into their own hands."

"We've spoken about it. There will be justice, real and proper justice, for Mark Voichek. Not street justice. It will wreck our cause if the citizens of the city think we're dangerous. Where are you going?"

"The home of Karl Poborski: 3238 Netherland Avenue in the Bronx."

"You've been a good friend to us. I'll talk to McAfferty and Doonz and the other vets and let you know when they're ready."

"There's no time. I'm heading there. If they're coming, tell them to get there as soon as they can."

29

───◆───

THE CAB SPED along the East River on the FDR Drive. The cabbie agreed to forgo the easy pickings of an Eastside St. Paddy's Day for the run to the Bronx after Taylor waved a twenty. The way he was tossing cash around, he'd already spent next week's pay on this story. Who was he kidding? The financial stakes were a lot higher than that. A multi-million-dollar city contract. Maybe more than one. It was enough to murder for. He was missing something though. What had been going on between McNally and Poborski the past five months?

From his pocket, he pulled a piece of wire copy from Mrs. Wiggins' desk. Huế, South Vietnam's third largest city, wouldn't last the week. Panicked people streamed south. When Huế fell, the Communists would point their invading column at Saigon. His brother's face, the teenaged Billy, not the soldier, came to mind. The man in uniform had faded from memory. Was he forgetting Billy's role as quickly as the country was forgetting its *bad* war? The face turned into Declan McNally's on the autopsy table. Finding the killer was supposed to get him his job back and ease the pain. Another bad plan.

The cab dropped him at the corner. He decided to stake out

the house and see if the murderers showed. Shadows passed back and forth behind the drapes of the bay window. *One man pacing? Two moving around? A party?* St. Paddy's Day wasn't celebrated in this house. He walked past, eyed the door and kept going until he was at the other corner. The black Olds was nowhere in sight. He chewed a fresh stick of Teaberry. Wintergreen crossed with licorice. The residential street offered nowhere out of sight to wait. It was also a watchful neighborhood. He hadn't been there ten minutes when a blue and white squad car pulled up.

The window slid down and an overweight patrolman with a mottled face asked, "You lost, buddy?"

"No, Officer. Just heading toward Broadway."

"Then head."

Taylor walked back on Netherland as the cruiser rolled alongside. It pulled away after they were five houses beyond Poborski's. He turned around and closed in on the front walk. *Abandon the stakeout and question Poborski?* He must. It was either that or get yanked on a loitering charge. He reached the front stoop and pressed the doorbell. As the button sunk under the pressure of his finger, his stomach tightened. He knew he'd set something in motion, something he wouldn't be able to stop. This was the story he had to get. He'd never faced an interview more important. Or more dangerous. He should be scared but he wasn't. He wanted this too badly. The bald-headed son, Sash, opened the door and glared. "What do you want?"

"I'd like to talk to your father."

"Who is it, Sash?" yelled Karl Poborski from down the hall.

"It's that reporter."

"Just a few follow-up questions." Taylor spoke over Sash's shoulder in the direction of the older man's voice.

"Don't be rude. By all means, invite him in."

Sash opened the storm door and led Taylor down the hallway past the living room to a big kitchen painted the color of lemon meringue. Something bubbled in a shiny steel pot on the stove. The stench of cabbage was stronger, if that was possible, and the place was still a hot house. Karl Poborski sat at the far end of a Formica table cleared but for two half-full coffee cups, two empty shot glasses, and a bottle of vodka. He was silhouetted against the darkened entrance to the dining room. Someone sat in there. Taylor couldn't make out details, just a presence. Outnumbered three to one. Not good. He hoped the homeless vets showed up soon.

"I'm sure we can be more hospitable this evening. Now is the time for men to do business, not during a family's Sunday dinner." Poborski lifted the bottle. "Can I offer you some?"

"Thanks, but no."

"It's not polite to let a man drink alone." He filled a glass near to brimming and sipped a little off the top. "You know the Russians even stole vodka from the Polish. We invented it. Such bastards."

Taylor sat in the chair nearest. "I have some questions about the salt contract."

"Is that so?" Poborski grinned like it was a punch line.

"Do you remember going to McNally's office after losing the contract?"

"No. Doesn't mean it didn't happen."

"It did. I'm told you were furious. You yelled at McNally so loudly everyone in the office could hear." Taylor read from his notebook. " 'We take care of each other. You remember that. Your fucking father-in-law knows. I guess you're not really *family,* are you?' "

"Tsk, tsk. Such language."

"You made a threat."

"I was angry, of course. I'm a competitive businessman. I was seeking a solution. That's all. No threat."

"So now you remember?"

"Why should I deny it? You have these wonderful sources." Poborski toasted with the shot glass.

"You brought McNally's family into it."

"It was crude. I admit that. I was simply pointing out that Mr. McNally married into a very powerful family. He is not *of* that family. You are making stories where there are none."

The mobster was casual and unworried. This was rolling off him. Taylor needed fast confirmation and some insurance if the vets didn't show to back him up. Time to spin out a story of his own.

"What about your calls to Lydia McNally? What is the 'arrangement' you had with McNally? What 'steps' are you going to take? I think I know. Soon after you spoke to her, three men showed up at Murphy's looking for McNally. You sent them. They're the same men who killed Mark Voichek. They're the same men who stole Voichek's clothing to use in the murder of Declan McNally. I've written the story. My editor is only holding it for your comment. I have half an hour. After that, it will run no matter what. And this story is going to run and run."

"I really was hoping you didn't know so much." Poborski waved his finger in a naughty boy gesture. "I've not dealt with reporters before. I didn't expect such diligence. This business is messy enough."

The figure in the dining room rose and entered the kitchen. A tall man with a thin, white scar on his face. He held the Fedora in his left hand. Taylor got to his feet. Sash blocked the route to the front door. Real confirmation of the story stood before him. Now if he could live long enough to *actually* write it. Bluff more and come up with enough of a plan to get out the door.

"You heard what I said. This is going in tomorrow's paper. It's page one stuff. It runs whether I call by deadline or not."

"You'll give new instructions," Poborski said.

"That's not going to happen."

Fedora stepped across the room and hit Taylor hard in the stomach, then again, harder. "Oh, you'll call."

Taylor's knees buckled as the air rushed out of his lungs. He slumped into the kitchen table, knocked the vodka bottle off and went down on his hands and knees gasping to breathe. The reek of vodka threatened to gag him even as he fought to pull in air.

"Spignolli, don't make a goddamn mess in my kitchen."

Taylor rolled over on his back and prayed for his diaphragm to stop its spasms. The .32 might improve the bad odds, but he had to get it out before Spignolli searched him.

"He must be convinced or that story will take care of us," Spignolli said.

"Go ahead and convince him, but if you spill the hulupki, *my wife* will take care of us."

Taylor curled up in a feigned coughing fit, and as he did, reached for the pistol grip. Spignolli was too fast. He kicked Taylor's wrist hard. Pain shot up his arm. The killer violently wrenched the gun from his hand. The pain doubled.

"A gun? What are you doing running around with this little popper?" Spignolli delivered a vicious kick to Taylor's head.

A white flash. Black.

He dropped to the bottom of a well. This was good. It was probably for the best that he stay down here and let things pass by up there in the light of the kitchen.

No, that was wrong. He had to be in the room. Even if the pain was there too.

He climbed out of the well in his aching skull and forced his eyes to open. The linoleum was cold against his cheek. The shiny toe of an expensive dress shoe came into view, and beyond that, fog. Men speaking. His ears worked better than his eyes for a reason he didn't understand. He wondered why that was the thing he chose to focus on. Didn't he have bigger concerns? Muddle and pain.

"Take him out the back through the porch. My neighbors are too nosey. Deal with him the right way. No more bodies dressed like the fucking homeless this time."

"I told you." Spignolli's anger was barely suppressed. "That worked for us before. No one ever thinks to dredge the cemetery."

"It fucking didn't work this time. And then you left that bum on the river. No wonder we've got this reporter on us like stink on shit. Get him out of here."

Spignolli pulled Taylor to his feet and pushed him toward the back door.

The rough jostling made his head hurt like he'd been kicked again.

"Jesus Fucking Christ, who's at the door now?"

That explained the chimes. Taylor assumed they were part of the ringing in his head.

"Sash, go."

Spignolli pushed open the back door and shoved. Taylor stumbled and sprawled on the ice-cold concrete floor. Shadows stooped in the corners of the porch. They didn't move, didn't stand, instead resolved into outdoor furniture.

Yelling followed by two shots.

"What the fuck?" Spignolli turned in the doorway, pulled out a large caliber revolver and disappeared back into the kitchen.

Taylor's vision cleared a little more, but his head throbbed as if his pulse were wired to a pain button. He rose to a crouch. Outside, beyond the porch, was Poborski's snow-covered backyard. A clothesline of two crossed pipes on a single pole. White rope hung with icicles. A birdbath was buried up to its bowl.

He moved back to the doorway into the kitchen. Two more gunshots, a guttural yell and a crash. The house must be under attack. Just his luck to confirm the story and end up in the middle of a mob war. His gun lay on the kitchen table. He scrambled across the empty room, grabbed it and crouched low in the porch doorway. He'd wait here until the shooting stopped. Dead reporters wrote no tales.

Spignolli ran back into the kitchen, stopped to fire a shot

down the hall and charged toward Taylor. Taylor backed onto the cement deck and held up his gun, which looked like a toy compared to Spignolli's magnum. Fear gripped the mobster's scarred face. The hit man wasn't coming for Taylor. He was running from someone. He turned in the doorway and shot wildly into the house.

An explosive crack in reply lifted Spignolli off his feet and threw him into Taylor with such force that Taylor fell back through the porch's screen door and into the snow.

His vision wobbled again from the kick he'd taken to the head. He scrambled to get to his feet, slipped on the snow, and got up again. Two hands grabbed him. They pulled him along the back of the house and around the side. Taylor struggled against arms of iron-cord muscle.

A whisper from behind. "Easy. Here to help."

Taylor turned to the homeless veteran, McAfferty. "Shit, you've got to stop appearing out of nowhere."

"Some firefight. What the fuck is going on in there?"

"Someone's after the murderers."

He crept to the corner of the house and looked around. A man stepped onto the porch and fired once more into Spignolli's prone body. The killer came off the porch and stopped on the steps with the gun at his side. The moon lit the snow and the man. Constable McNally checked the yard and went back inside. Taylor had it wrong. This was no mob war. This was revenge.

"Doonz and some others are nearby, but we're not messing with guns. We need to move out." As if in answer to McAfferty, sirens wailed from the direction of 254th Street. "I ain't spending time in a cube. We're just the folks the cops like to pull after something messy like this. Quick arrests are the best kind. Sort 'em all out later."

They edged along the wall. A car roared to life on the street. Taylor couldn't help but run forward to get a look.

"Jesus, Taylor. No."

He reached the sidewalk as a light blue Lincoln leaped from the curb with a squeal. McNally was at the wheel. The pain in Taylor's head almost beat him to the snowy ground. The sirens moved closer, and there were more of them.

"We're pulling out." McAfferty's voice dropped as he moved away. "Take care of yourself."

"You too." Taylor didn't blame McAfferty. He and his buddies *should* fear the NYPD.

He went to the front door of the house. Sash was sprawled in the doorway, his eyes open and his tongue lolling out of his mouth. He'd been shot once in the forehead as he opened the door. Poborski was farther down the hall, on his back, with gunshot wounds to the chest and face. Also dead. The sweet iron aroma of the blood mixed with the sour cabbage.

On the porch, Spignolli's lip quivered. He breathed through spittle, like he was sipping tea. His eyes closed and his breathing grew shallower. Taylor didn't think he'd last much longer.

He had to get going. In another two hours, every police reporter in town would know about the killings at the house. After that, the whole story would spill. He couldn't afford to spend that time being questioned by cops.

He walked out through the porch and struggled to move quickly through the backyards of Riverdale to Johnson Avenue, holding his wrist, which was swelling and now hurt almost as much as his head. His pants were soaked through. Three patrol cars flew down Johnson and screeched as they turned onto 230th to cut over to Netherland. Nausea from the blow to his head flipped his stomach once, twice, but he kept lunch down somehow. He shook from the cold. He only had a couple bucks left. Didn't matter. There were no cabs on Broadway anyway.

He went to a pay phone in the subway station and called Inspector Dellossi. A detective on the McNally detail took the call and said Dellossi was out.

"Tell him it's about the shootings at the Poborski house in the Bronx."

"What shootings?"

"Check the radio, man. Two dead, maybe three. Constable McNally did it, in retribution for the murder of his son. You need to get people after McNally."

"How do you know this?"

A train braked on the downtown side of the tracks.

"Tell Dellossi I'm writing the story. He can call me if he wants to know what I know. I'll be at my desk in forty minutes."

He hung up and just made the 1 train as the doors clattered shut. Here was where police work and newspaper work took separate paths. The cops had their job to pursue McNally, arrest him, and charge him with killing the mobsters in revenge. The poor bastard. He'd lost his son and now faced long jail time. All because he took some money for city contracts. That was a sad story, tragic even. Readers would eat it up. Taylor had to somehow get this in the paper by deadline. After that, the press pack would tear away at the story, his advantage gone.

Dellossi was going to be pissed off, probably pissed off enough to drag him out of the newsroom. That was okay. He'd get to the *MT* just in time for Worthless to try and fire him.

30

———◆———

Taylor stepped off the elevator into a newsroom electric with the energy of a deadline. Every typewriter rattled at once. Reporters walked just at the edge of running. Worthless sat in the slot, editing. Oscar Garfield stood next to the City Desk reading typescript.

"Mr. Garfield, I've got a good one for tomorrow," Taylor said.

Worth eyed Taylor like lunch. "It's five fifteen. You missed our meeting. Not to worry. You're still fired."

"For once, you might want to listen to a reporter." Taylor turned to address Garfield. "Constable McNally just shot the men who murdered his kid. At least two dead. A mobster named Poborski and his son. Corruption in city contracting. I'm naming names. Names make news." The last line was the editor-in-chief's favorite slogan. If there was a time to sell a story, it was now.

"I don't care if you saw Jimmy Hoffa do it," said Worth. "You're done—"

"Wait a minute." Garfield held up his hand. "Big Johnny's son-in-law committed murder?"

"For revenge. I was there. I have a firsthand account *and*

Poborski's last interview. Declan's killers worked for him."

"Please remember this is Taylor." Worth stood. "He should never have been on this. How do we even know it's true?"

"Easy enough. We check it out." Garfield picked up the phone. He looked at Taylor. "Where was this?"

"Three two three eight Netherland Avenue in Riverdale."

"Who's in the cop shop? Hello, Fahey. Anything going on in the Bronx?" The editor-in-chief kept his eyes on Taylor as he spoke into the receiver. "Where was the triple? Any idea what happened?" He hung up the phone. "Three dead at that address, including a mob guy named Karl Poborski. Nobody knows why. You have this exclusive?"

"No one else is on it. It also ties into the death of Mark Voichek."

Garfield folded his arms and looked across the newsroom. The editor-in-chief liked scoops more than anything else in the world.

"How can he do a story?" Worth licked his lips. "We fired him."

"He still works for me through today's deadline, right?"

"Well, I guess, but—"

"I'll give it that long. Type up what you've got. If it proves out, we'll see what happens next."

"You got it." Taylor started for his desk.

"Absolutely no mistakes."

"No. None."

He might be head, leg, and arm sore, but he had a deadline for a good story. The ultimate painkiller. When he got to his desk, a sheet of copy paper had been paper rolled into the Selectric. A typed note from Laura. There was also a manila envelope propped on the keys. He pulled out the note.

> Dick B. took the pix in this envelope about three months ago outside an apartment on East 30th. Declan convinced Dick to follow Constable. He told Dick he

wanted shots for a "This Is Your Life" surprise album for Daddy's birthday.

Once he got them, Dick realized that was a lie and Declan planned to blackmail his father. Declan confirmed this after Dick gave him the pix. He kept this one set of prints. He's a pretty scared kid.

Taylor stopped reading to pull out the photos. They were Exhibit A in a divorce proceeding. Black and whites of Constable McNally in various passionate embraces with a blond woman. In the last one, with a full view of her face, Taylor realized the woman was Celebration Jones, Big Johnny's mistress. His heart thudded in his ears. He read the rest of the note.

Here's a quote from Bennett we can use:

When I gave the pictures to him, Declan whistled and smiled weirdly. He said, 'Daddy, Daddy. What would Grandfather say?' He yelled at me for not staying longer and getting more indecent poses. I said I don't do that sort of thing. This was supposed to be a birthday surprise, not something nasty. He tried to pay me two hundred for them. I don't need money. I didn't want any money for doing something like this. Now I don't know what's going on.

I waited for you but it's getting close to deadline. I'm going to take a couple of the pics and ask McNally what was going on between him and his son.
—LW

He read those last two sentences again. Fear ripped through him. Laura was on her way to McNally's townhouse to question him about the blackmail.

He dialed and demanded Dellossi get on the phone.

"I've sent a squad to bring you in. Do not fucking move."

"Don't care about that. Are detectives on their way to McNally's house?"

"Why would I do that on your word alone? You make shit up."

"Jesus Christ, Dellossi. He shot three men. Laura Wheeler is headed over there to talk to him. She doesn't know what he did. Declan was blackmailing his father. We've got the pictures. She's going to show them to him. What do you think he's going to do then?"

"You come in here and explain your whole big story to me. I love a good tale."

Taylor hung up. He ran the zigzag path from obits to Garfield's office.

"Laura's in trouble. She's on her way to McNally's. Declan was blackmailing his father over an affair. "

"How do you know?"

"We have pictures."

"Did you tell the police?"

"Fucking useless."

"What about the story?"

"This *is* the story. I'll phone it in if I can."

"No, Taylor. This is for the police— Goddammit, Taylor—."

He didn't hear the rest. He didn't care if he lost his job five minutes after getting it back. He was in a near panic when he got out to 28th. He'd been behind on this story the entire time. He knew what McNally would do when confronted with those pictures. He'd killed already.

Taylor had the story all wrong. Now Laura faced a murderer. He couldn't lose her.

A checker cab with an off-duty light came down the street. He stepped out to block its path. Tires squealed.

"Goddammit. Are you crazy, man?"

"Twenty bucks to Sixty-ninth off First." Twenty bucks he didn't have.

"I'm off duty."

"Thirty. Keep it off the meter." Easy to bid it up when he didn't have it. "I'll throw in another ten if you get me there in less than ten minutes."

"Get in."

The cabbie jumped lights and blew stale yellows to pull to the front of the McNally townhouse in what Taylor clocked at nine minutes.

"Thanks. Wait for me."

"I'm done tonight, man. Pay me now."

"Don't have it. You're going to have to wait if you want the money."

"You are *not* jumping a forty dollar fare."

"Report it then. There's a guy with a gun inside here, so if you could call that in too, I might live long enough to pay you."

"What a shitty night. Drunks and crazies. I hate St. Patrick's Day."

Taylor didn't wait to see what the cabbie did. The door to the townhouse was ajar. He eased it open. Two more adultery photos lay on the floor as if dropped there. He picked them up. On the wall, a framed black-and-white photo of cops in old-fashioned uniforms hung lopsided. The glass in a second frame was cracked. Between them, a smear of blood on the wall. There had been a struggle here.

Please just let Laura be all right. The story didn't matter. Nothing else mattered. Taylor pulled the .32 out of the holster.

He crept down the dark hallway. At the back of the house, music played. He checked the living room, which was dark and empty. On a side table sat a glass that gave off the sharp bite of whisky straight.

The music increased in volume as he approached Declan McNally's rumpus room. It turned into a distinct song. Irish voices sang a chorus about a whistling gypsy.

The room appeared little changed from his earlier visit. The television was tuned to *The Merv Griffin Show*, and a stereo turntable by the wall nearest him spun an album. The song finished, the tone arm lifted automatically, glided over the LP and started playing the same record again. He came around the back of the wingback chair. Laura sat in it with her hands tied in front of her. A trickle of blood ran from her hairline down the side of her face, which was tinged red. She looked at him with relief. He almost hugged her right then but checked himself. First he had to make sure she wasn't badly hurt.

"Are you all right?" He dropped the gun into his jacket pocket and stooped down to untie the cord cutting into her wrists.

"It's him," she whispered. "We've got to get out of here."

"I know." He squeezed her hands lightly. "How bad are you?"

"I showed him the pictures. He hit me hard. Right out of the blue. I crashed into the wall. I hurt here." Her hands free now, she pointed to the side of her head. "Could be a lot worse."

"McNally?"

"He went to get his gun."

"He killed Poborski." Taylor untied her ankles from the chair legs. She stood and immediately slumped into him, and he held her up.

"Still dizzy."

"Let's go."

"Taylor!" She gripped his arms hard, and he thought she was going to swoon into dead weight. Cold metal pressed the back of his neck.

"She said you knew about the pictures." McNally was right behind him. "I wasn't sure if that was true, so I'm so glad you came. It's good we're all here together."

"Easy, McNally. We don't need any more bodies tonight. I'm going to let Laura sit." He pulled slowly away from the gun barrel, lowered her to the chair and turned around with his hands out in front.

"Over there." McNally pointed to the couch with a .38 police service revolver. His other hand held a whisky. He gulped it like a thirsty man drinking water. "Both reporters. This completes my night."

"Let us go, McNally."

"Why would I do that?" The barrel of the gun drew lazy circles in the air.

Taylor took one end of the couch, his legs tensed to spring when he saw an opening. "We're not cops. We're not going to stop you. Take off. Go anywhere you like."

"You're fucking worse than cops. I really thought I'd taken care of things with Poborski. The detectives were going to believe my story. I'm one of them. I'd get off. I'd be a goddamn hero, but this bitch shows up with those pictures."

"You know *this bitch* left pictures back in the newsroom, right?" Laura asked.

"I'll fix that."

The man was drunk and on the edge. He'd just shot three people.

Keep him talking and wait for a chance. That was Taylor's only option. Focus like this was the last story he'd ever do. Or it would be. "Why was your son blackmailing you?"

"I get it. A last interview. *Your* last interview. Sure, why not?" McNally moved over by the stereo, probably to get the best angle on both of them. He swallowed another gulp of whisky. "If you haven't figured it out yet, my boy wasn't a good boy. Not just bad. Evil. Black hearted."

"What did he want from you?"

"What? Why, everything. Oh he said he was angry with me for cheating on his mother. Who he loved so very dearly. He said I needed to be punished. All lies." McNally laughed without mirth. "My son loved no one. He *got* money from me. A car. That wasn't enough. More money every month. He kept at me no matter what I did. He required I pump the guys on the force for info to help him expand his drug business at

Columbia. If I didn't help him, he threatened to destroy my marriage, my career. My whole life. I know Big Johnny. That fat fuck would wreck me if he saw those photos. Me with *his* woman. Me cheating on *his* little girl. It's okay for him to do it. Just not me. Then two weeks ago, Declan announced we were done. He was going to give the pictures to Big Johnny, no matter what I did. No matter what I paid. He said he needed to be free of me. He said the only thing he wanted was nothing. To bring on anarchy. Anarchy? What the fuck does that mean? I took care of the problem. I couldn't let him tear everything down. He was a monster out to destroy everything I'd built. I couldn't let that happen."

"How did Poborski get involved?"

"That made perfect sense." McNally spoke like a man sure of his logic. "I asked Poborski for his help because he'd lost the contract. No one would suspect me of working with the loser. I told him I'd help him out if he fixed my problem. He fucked up. Didn't want to get his hands dirty. Too much of a big shot. Big shot? An old Polock fuck. He picked Spignolli and that moron got cute with the drugs and the homeless clothes. Believe me, it's not because you're so damn smart." He pointed the gun at Taylor. "It was fucking stupidity that got you sniffing around. As it turned out, I couldn't get him the salt contract back. Hell, I figured he'd take another bone once we were in business together. It wasn't as big, but it was money. The big shot didn't like that. He went nuts about trust. Mobsters and their fucking trust. He threatened me. He threatened my wife. He threatened to go to Big Johnny. I had to end that too."

"You don't want two dead reporters. The pictures are in the newsroom. How are you ever going to make this fly?"

"I'll figure out a good story. I like this life."

He leveled the gun at Taylor. It stopped wavering.

A bottle exploded against the side of McNally's head. A big shard of glass with a Smirnoff's label landed in Taylor's lap. The revolver went off.

The gagging smell of vodka again.

"You like this life!" screamed Lydia from the doorway to the rumpus room. "How do you think you got this life? You bastard. You killed my son. You killed him."

McNally staggered and somehow kept on his feet. His first shot had gone wild, through the window over the couch.

He trained the revolver on his wife's face. "What the fuck?" McNally sounded bewildered as blood poured down his face. "Honey, you usually sleep when you take your pills."

Taylor pulled the .32 from his pocket, took a step to make sure of his aim and shot McNally in the right shoulder. He spun back toward Taylor. McNally yelled in pain and fell to the carpet, grabbing at his shoulder. Taylor took the gun out of McNally's limp hand. Lydia McNally kicked her husband in the back and howled something unintelligible. Taylor pulled her away by the shoulders.

She shook loose and wandered down the hall. "I need another bottle. I broke my damn bottle."

A crash from the kitchen.

He checked McNally. His eyes were alive and full of rage. He moved over and crouched in front of Laura. "How are you doing?"

"A little less dizzy. With one serious adrenaline high."

Taylor looked at his watch.

"How much time?"

"Twenty-five minutes until the three-star edition closes."

Sirens pulled up out front. He sat down on the couch and dialed the city desk. Laura joined him. She looked exhausted but offered a little smile.

"I've got one for you, Mr. Garfield. Have you got a slot?"

"I put an AP story out of Saigon into a hole on page one in case you didn't make it in time."

"What's the Saigon story?"

"We don't have time."

"Just tell me what it is."

"Another big town fell. The whole country's going into the toilet. Same old same old."

Same old same old. Billy would be buried forever under the same old same old.

"How long?"

"Twenty column inches if we get this to the shop floor in seventeen, no sixteen minutes. That's drop dead."

"It's not much space."

"Write a goddamn follow-up tomorrow. Go."

"All right. This won't be same old same old. Byline, C.S. Taylor and Laura Wheeler." Laura squeezed his arm hard and held on. "Dateline, Manhattan. First graph, City attorney Constable McNally ordered a mob hit on his son, Declan, to stop the sixteen-year-old from blackmailing him over an affair with a mistress the senior McNally shared with his father-in-law, Manhattan Democratic party boss John Scudetto."

Garfield whistled low. "This is good, Taylor. You can come see me tomorrow." Ambulance men started working on McNally, who groaned and swore. Somewhere down the hall, Lydia McNally yelled obscenities at a policeman.

"Second graph."

In ten minutes, Taylor had dictated twenty column inches to the word. He pulled Voichek's obit out of his pocket.

"I've got one more thing for tomorrow's paper."

Photo by Domenica Comfort

RICH ZAHRADNIK HAS been a journalist for 30-plus years, working as a reporter and editor in all major news media, including online, newspaper, broadcast, magazine, and wire services.

Zahradnik held editorial positions at CNN, *Bloomberg News*, Fox Business Network, AOL, and the *Hollywood Reporter*, often writing news stories and analysis about the journalism business, broadcasting, film production, publishing, and the online industry. In January 2012, he was one of 20 writers selected for the inaugural class of the Crime Fiction Academy, a first-of-its-kind program run by New York's Center for Fiction.

A media entrepreneur throughout his career, he was founding executive producer of CNNfn.com, a leading financial news website and a Webby winner; managing editor of Netscape.com, and a partner in the soccer news website company, Goal Networks. Zahradnik also co-founded the weekly newspaper, the *Peekskill Herald*, at the age of 25, leading it to seven state press association awards in its first three years.

Zahradnik was born in Poughkeepsie, New York, and received his B.A. in journalism and political science from George Washington University. He lives with his wife Sheri and son Patrick in Pelham, New York, where he teaches elementary school kids how to publish online and print newspapers.

For more information, go to www.richzahradnik.com.